COURT OF SHADOWS

FORBIDDEN MAGIC BOOK ONE

K.N. LEE

CAPTIVE QUILL PRESS

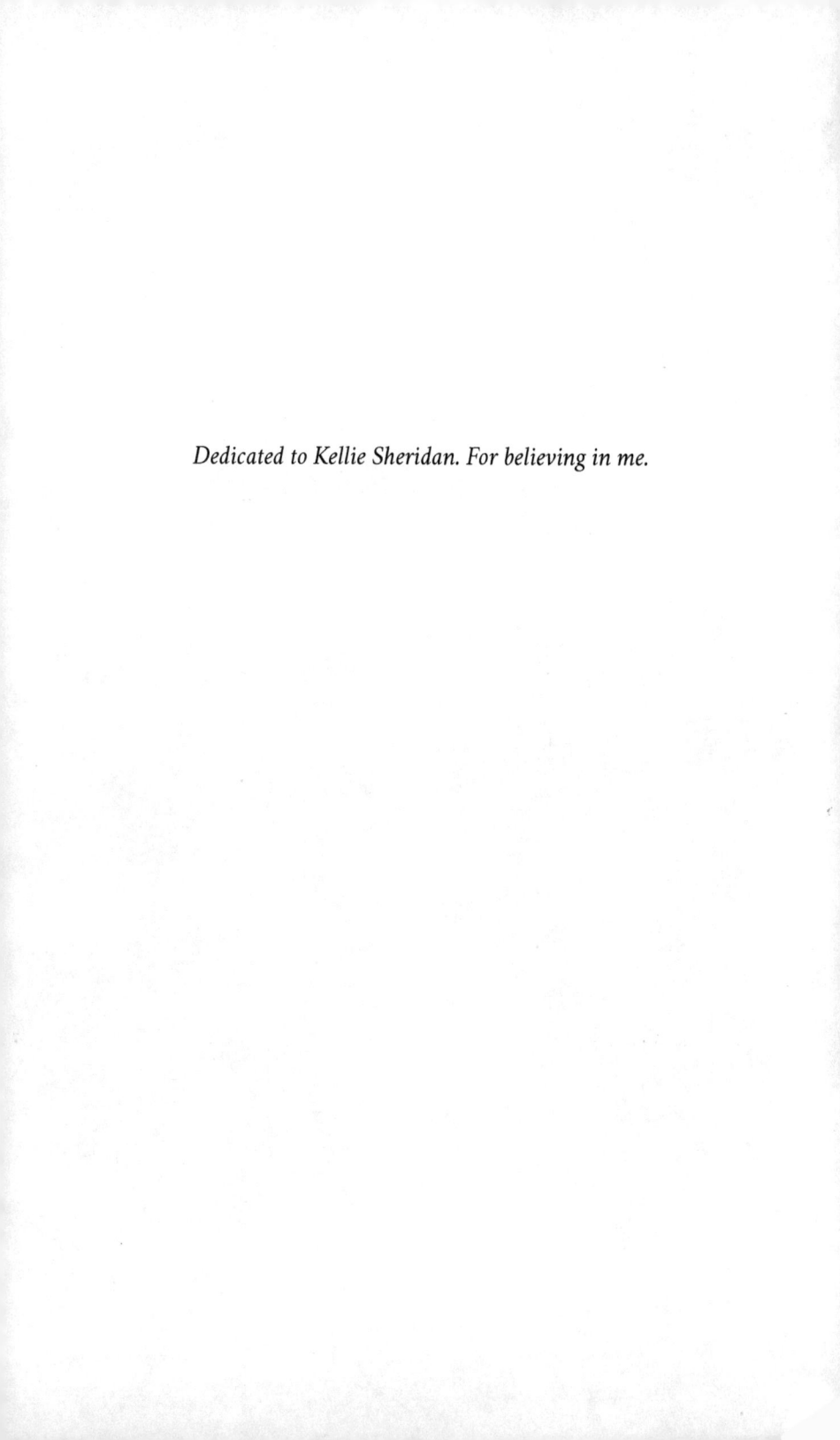

Dedicated to Kellie Sheridan. For believing in me.

FOREWORD

I am pleased and excited to present the first book in the Forbidden Magic series. I did, however, want to make sure I explained its origins.

I wrote this story years ago, and it has evolved into an epic world that is connected to the Eura Chronicles universe. You may be familiar with Lilae and Liam from Rise of the Flame, and Preeti and Vineet from Goddess of War. Now, I introduce Celeste and her court of four intriguing princes.

In this story, you'll be able to get the point of view of each main character. When you see the beginning of the chapter say, The Aether, that is from Celeste's point of view. The Earth Prince, is Maxim's. And, so forth.

I do hope you enjoy this new series.

Until next time,
K.N. Lee

THE WORLDS OF RUNE

THE SEELIE COURT

Allandria-Center of the Seelie Court and home to the Elemental Throne
Ostrum- Faun and Elven Kingdom
Brytania- Gnome and Selkie Kingdom
Erun- Angel Kingdom
Ever Frost- Giant Kingdom

THE UNSEELIE COURT

Mordigan-Center of the Unseelie Court
Asha- Elven Kingdom
Cartania- Changeling Kingdom
Inaeza- Dragon Kingdom
Ever Bloom- Pixie, Nymph, and Sprite Kingdom

THE HUMAN REALM

Tythra

Kyushu

Heryni

Anatolia

Londinium

THE DEAD REALM

The Veil- Boundary that separates the living from the dead

Mestos

Pothos

Rosthos

Aesthos

THE Elementals

The Earth Prince- Maxim

The Water Prince- Stellan

The Air Prince- Ewan

The Fire Prince- Lancel

The Aether- Celeste

CHAPTER 1

"You may not see us, but we are there; watching you, protecting you, and fighting the darkness that wants your soul."

The Aether

From the prison window, I looked out to the dark world that stretched for miles below.

The Crimson Tower had been home for eleven years, and each year I beheld the same bleak landscape.

Snow. Ice. Darkness.

Sometimes the wind would howl so loudly that the echo on the stone walls would keep me awake for hours. In this part of the realm, the sun barely shed more than a faint hue in the gray sky as thick clouds seemed to hover and drift along at a slow crawl.

Not even the fire could warm me, and even though I'd been born in a hot summer surrounded by tropical jungles, I'd grown used to being cold—to being alone.

Mother had always told me that one day life would change, that I would be free.

Maybe even more than free.

That was before the humans had taken her and father away and burned them at the stake—before my grandmother convinced King Aerion to imprison me instead of executing me. No one found it particularly becoming of a man to kill a little girl, especially when she had yet to display any signs that she'd inherited the stain of magic.

He had agreed. But, the fear of death hovered above me like a black cloud.

Even as I finished hanging my washing above the fire, I wasn't sure what to expect when the sound of horses broke me from my daydream. The heat did little to warm my face as I dried my wet hands on my apron.

For years, I had watched the world below churn with snow and darkness. But, that night, there was light.

I pushed open the window and shivered at the bitter wind as it swept in and lifted my golden hair. To my relief, it wasn't the king's soldiers.

It was a carriage of black and gold.

I leaned out the window, gawking at how the embellishments glittered beneath the bright moon.

"Look, Kala. You don't see one of those every day," I muttered.

"Indeed," Kala, the white dire wolf at my side agreed. "Not in the Outlands of Tythra, anyway."

In the midst of a snowstorm, a beautiful woman stepped from the covered carriage in a gray fur cloak with a wolf's head that reached the ankles of her black boots. She didn't walk to the entrance of the Crimson Tower.

She flew.

Her long hair cascaded down her back in red waves, and her green eyes glittered beneath her lashes. Even in the dark, I could see them, for they glowed up at me.

"I've yet to see a human fly, or do anything interesting for that matter," Kala said.

"A faerie," I said, eyes wide with awe. "Someone will surely kill her for showing off magic in such a way. How is this possible?"

"We will have to see," Kala said. "Perhaps they have summoned her."

"Unlikely," I said, closing the shutters against the cold. I leaned back onto the wall, wondering if this was a dream. "Do you think it could be her?"

"We can only hope," Kala said, glancing up at me with ice-blue eyes that sparkled in the dim candlelight. "Eleven years is far too long for anyone to lose their freedom."

"I almost don't want to get my hopes up," I said, taking off my apron and hanging it on a hook behind the door. "I don't think I could take such a disappointment."

"Don't give up hope, darling. All will work itself out. I promise."

With my ear pressed to the door, I tried to listen in on what she said to the warden. It was fruitless. I was high up in the tower, and the stone door was thick enough to mute all sounds from the corridor.

The locked clicked. I jumped and took a frightened step back.

Frozen, my eyes darted from one armored guard to the next. With their swords pointed my way, and shields held out to block whatever they feared I would do to them, I realized they were afraid of me.

That was odd. Why would anyone fear me? A more pressing question came to me as the guards made a passage in between them.

"Come, girl," one of them demanded. "Warden says you're being released."

Those seven words more than those two guards had ever said to me.

Still, I couldn't move. All I could do was look to my right at the only window in the room and to my left. This had been my home since I was seven years old. My meager bed was pushed against the wall to give myself more space for my desk and bookcase. It was all I had in the entire world, but none of it mattered anymore.

Freedom potentially waited for me.

Kala stood beside me. While I tried to keep my fear at bay, there was strength and courage in her eyes.

"Are you ready?" Kala asked, startling the guards with her soft voice that echoed off the walls.

Though they remained silent, their eyes widened with questions I knew they were asking themselves.

Licking my cracked lips, I nodded despite the pain of the sting I'd awakened. "I think so."

I mustered my courage and stepped from my tiny prison. The cold followed me outside into the corridor as we walked along the narrow hall to the staircase that led to the bottom of the tower.

There she was. The faerie. My heart skipped a beat as I remembered her face from long ago. The memory of her having tea with mother and father just the night before their arrest returned to me.

"My goodness," she said. "What a lovely little lady you've grown up to be. Come, let me get a better look at you."

Nervous and tense, I almost smiled at the compliment. But, the truth was, I wasn't sure how to feel. I took another step forward, and she touched my hair, her eyes examining every inch of my face.

"Do you remember me? I am Queen Sorcha of Ever Frost."

"Of course, I remember you. How could I forget?"

She'd taken a sample of my blood with the tip of her enchanted dagger. A little girl would never forget such a thing, no matter how much time had passed. I could still feel the sting and recall the way the blade glowed once it touched my blood, soaking it in as though quenched a desperate thirst.

"The war is over, and you are free to leave."

My knees buckled, and with widened eyes, my breaths quickened. "Are you certain?"

"I am," she said, stepping closer and taking my hands into hers. She stared down at them, stroking my rough skin with her thumbs. "I am sorry for how you've been mistreated, and how many years you've been forced to remain here. But, we have fought long and hard with the Tythrans to get you back. And, we've won."

Picturing armies of magic-born fighting against humans left my stomach in knots. "They fought...for me?"

"Of course, they did. And now, I will take you to where you belong. To Allandria, the center of the Seelie Court."

When I noticed that the warden and the guards were nowhere to be seen I knew it to be true. Despite my wariness, I nodded and was spirited away out into the cold. I did not ask questions, or delay my escape.

No. I was ready.

Whatever was before me would be better than a life of imprisonment. With Kala by my side, I climbed into the carriage and was wrapped in a heavy fur cloak.

If I was dreaming, I did not want to wake up ever again. I was free for the first time since I was a child. Even though I was about to be taken to a land I'd never seen other than in the books my grandmother had sent to me, I did not care.

A cold night with snow falling in torrents was the setting for my journey into the darkness of my fated future. My destiny. It was the day of my eighteenth birthday when the beautiful faerie queen took me away from the Crimson Tower.

My heart continued to race, and my muscles remained tense even as Kala snuggled close and kept me warm—even as we said goodbye to Tythra.

The humans were never my tribe, and each day on their soil was one day closer to my death.

No, I wasn't born to die such an uneventful death. I'd come from a long line of faeries with immortal blood running through their veins.

I was Princess Celeste Delacord of the kingdom of Mordigan —an Elemental chosen by the Guardians despite my heritage.

The first ever with the power to control all of the elements. Perhaps the humans were justified in my imprisonment, for it was prophecized that I could build or destroy nations with a single thought.

As we rode away, I glanced back at the tower, wondering when any of that power would give me a sign it even existed.

CHAPTER 2

The Water Prince

Morning brought with it a cool breeze from the open shutters of my private quarters. Outside, the snow-capped mountains awaited, with waterfalls of ice, and sparkling trees aglitter with tiny icicles that resembled precious stones.

I yawned, not yet ready to leave the comfort of my bed, or the warmth of the pretty Duchess of Kyrin.

As my manservant prepared my bath, I rolled onto my side and watched her sleep. She was a lovely young woman, but this would be the last time she'd share my bed. I was promised to another, and though I never believed she'd make it past her eighteenth birthday, she was now being rescued from a human prison.

Eliza opened her eyes, bright purple, with flecks of brown. She sat up, covering her perky breasts and gave me that alluring grin that had hooked me the moment she and her husband were presented at court last spring.

"Well, good morning, your highness," she purred, leaning down to kiss my forehead, then my mouth.

"Stellan," I said, as always. But, she insisted on calling me by my proper title.

While Jethroe prepared my clothes for the day, Eliza gave me a naughty wink and straddled me, her warm thighs on either side of my naked chest.

"Tell me it isn't so," she said, her sky-blue waves falling over her bony shoulders. As the blanket fell, her wings flapped like those of a hummingbird behind her.

"And, what is that?" I asked, squeezing her supple, pale thighs.

"That I'll lose you to a dark faerie, an Unseelie whore."

Tensing, I glared up at her. I wasn't a saint, and neither was she, but we knew what we were getting ourselves into. She was married to an old Duke with two other wives, and I was promised to another the day I was born.

"That's enough, Eliza. She will be your queen someday, and you will bow to her like everyone else in the realm."

She crossed her arms over her chest. "I will not. No one wants to see a filthy Unseelie on the Allandrian throne. It is a disgrace to us all."

That's it. I shoved her off of me.

I wasn't sure why her words triggered my wrath, but I left her in bed, confused, as I stalked across my bedroom to my bath.

"Fine, then," she cried after me. "March off to the whore of the magic-realm and pledge your life as her pet. See if I care."

I shook my head at Jethroe who chuckled behind his hand, and stepped into the pool of hot, scented water.

"That's right," I said. "And, you return to that crotchety old husband of yours."

I heard something crash and break, flinching, and then footsteps followed by the slamming of a door. I didn't want our tryst to end that way, but fate had already planned out my future, and Celeste meant more to me than Eliza ever could.

Waving Jethroe away, I sank into the water, arms outstretched over the sides and closed my eyes. Water was my element, and it recharged my strength and power. It also brought me solitude and calmed my nerves.

I needed it as my rage bubbled within.

Celeste wasn't a whore. She was an Elemental, like myself, and though I hadn't seen her in over eleven years, I'd loved her since the day we met.

After my bath, I met up with Prince Maxim in the great hall. He gave me a stern look from under long, disheveled brown hair. By the red-rim around his eyes, I knew what he'd been up to all night.

More studying.

The earth Elemental was the most boring person in the entire realm.

"Took you long enough," he said, clasping his hands behind his back.

I held my arms out as Jethroe put on my cloak and tied it at my throat, rolling my eyes.

"Patience is a virtue, isn't that right, Maxim?"

He smirked. "You know nothing of patience, my friend."

"Eager to meet our beloved Aether, are you?"

Looking down, I knew the answer. While myself and the other Elementals were enjoying our childhoods, he shared more in common with the Aether than any of us. While she was imprisoned, he'd been smuggled away and left in an orphanage to protect his identity.

I'd never forget the day my mother brought the orphan prince to our palace. As teenagers, we'd become fast friends.

I never cared that he was half-human.

"I am," he said, softly. "For years, she was so close that our power cried for one another. Now, I get to finally meet her."

Clasping a hand onto his shoulder, I nodded. "I know. We shall be in Allandria soon. But, first, I want to visit the Trials. I've heard reports of dark magic."

Maxim lifted a thick brow over pale green eyes. "You don't think—"

"I do," I said, leading the way out of the palace doors where our horses awaited. "There's evil afoot, and I'd have it banished before we depart."

CHAPTER 3

We left the palace early, prepared to visit the Trials before our departure. Of course, nothing ever went the way I'd planned. The airships were ready and stocked with everything we needed for the journey, but the crew would have to wait.

I was the heir to the Ever Frost throne, and the protector of the realm.

Set between two rows of buildings that reached as tall as the dark storm clouds above, the central market of Ever Frost filled the city's square. The glass dome that covered the inner city protected us from the extreme cold and the elements of our world's unrelenting foul weather.

The smell was what overwhelmed me at first. Spices and perfumes, raw fish and sweat. Fresh fruits and vegetables grown from genetic farms, raw or smoked meats, exotic smelling salts, carpets, and silks were all spread out over wooden tables draped with cloth and carts that had been pushed from far below the city's boundaries.

I was supposed to leave for Allandria that morning, but reports of a disturbance in my kingdom delayed my departure.

Eleven years had passed since I'd first met the Aether, what was another few days?

Maxim walked closely beside me, tall like a bodyguard, though I was the more muscular of the two of us. We were a good team, almost like brothers. After my mother rescued him from the orphanages in the human realm, he'd been stuck to me, almost like a shadow.

The prince of Ever Frost and the human prince without a kingdom. Still, as Elementals, we were bound by magic and couldn't escape one another if we tried.

I stroked my bearded chin as I glanced from building to building. The stone structures had been built centuries ago, and housed the faeries of Ever Frost. This was the most brutal terrain out of all of the realms, and yet, we'd found a way to survive.

Maxim walked slowly, carefully surveying our surroundings as we walked the stone streets and weaved our way in and out of the gathering crowds.

"Let me know if you notice anything out of the ordinary."

I nodded, not really paying attention to what he had said. My mind had already wandered to the large crowds of people that had come from all over the realm to witness the Trials—a series of tests for the warriors who were in a competition to serve the new queen once she arrived.

"Are you listening to me, Stellan? Of course, you aren't," he said, folding his arms across his chest. "Your heads in the clouds, as always."

"Yes, Maxim. I'm listening," I lied. "I'm also trying to focus. You should too."

"Something is not right," he whispered, tensing, his brows furrowing. He bent to take a handful of dirt from the side of the road where flowers and small trees had been planted.

I stood by as he sniffed the dark soil and glanced up at me with a scowl on his face. It wasn't much different from his usual expression.

Always serious, always a scholar, Maxim rarely smiled, but something about the glint of worry in his eyes worried me.

"What is it?"

He shook his head, standing to his full height which was nearly a half-foot taller than me.

"I'm not sure. Smells of something not of this world. I think its the faint scent of magic from The Veil," he said, scratching his chin. "I vaguely remember that strange aromas from crossing it years back."

"Just brilliant," I mumbled. That's all I needed was to deal with one of the creatures from The Veil stalking my kingdom.

We were both in disguise, wearing gray cloaks over our fine clothes. As we walked through the maze of streets and market-places, I tried to keep my hair covered, for red was rare in Ever Frost.

My mother was from a faraway kingdom, where such a shade was more common. But, here, the faeries were more used to white or blond hair, with the occasional bright blue like Eliza's.

"The reports say there is a possible body snatcher lingering about," Maxim said.

My cheeks paled. This was something beyond my training. "A corsus?"

He nodded, confirming my fear of the evil creatures who liked to steal and inhabit the bodies of those of weak body or mind.

"Why couldn't it be something simple, like a sprite? Sprites are at least easy to banish back to The Veil."

He shrugged, lifting a thick brow. "Sprites don't like the cold."

Bloody know-it-all. I scowled over my shoulder. "That wasn't a literal question, my friend. I just wish it would be something easy and not a class 5 entity."

"I see," Maxim said, his voice lowering. "The patrollers count seven bodies left behind."

I shook my head, and began to take a step forward when Maxim stopped me by outstretching his arm in my path.

"Wait," he said. "Do you smell that?"

I sniffed the air. The faint scent of death wafted over the collection of usual aromas of the morning market.

"Death," I said, throwing open my cloak to reveal a scepter made of bone, onyx, and enchanted glass.

Maxim glanced at me. "You ready?"

I stretched my neck muscles from side to side. "Always."

CHAPTER 4

The Earth Prince

W hile Prince Stellan held out his scepter, I cracked my knuckles and summoned the energy of the earth around us.

All went silent, and the air grew heavy and thick.

The threads of the universe were corded beneath the stone, and soil, and I connected to them with my mental energy. The sensation of warmth and tingling sparks of magic vibrated up from the soles of my boots to the top of my head.

The environment spoke to me like an old, intimate friend, whispering, brushing my cheek.

If anything was amiss, I would feel it.

A whistling sound made Stellan and I pause. The market square quieted as everyone turned to look up at the sky.

Six armored, winged, Wind-Walkers flew from the south of the city and stopped in formation above us. With their swords held upward with the silver blades resting against their shoulders, they hovered in the air, patrolling the entire square.

"They really didn't spare any expense for the Trials," Stellan said, glancing up at them.

"More faeries means more security is needed," I said, not forgetting our mission.

If a corsus was in the city, it needed to be removed. We had a journey to Allandria to begin, and both Stellan and I if were eager to meet the young Unseelie faerie who would be queen. I'd dreamed of her since I was a young lad, cold, and lonely even though I was surrounded by hundreds of orphans. I dare say, the thought of her alone was what helped me survive.

The sound of drums drew my attention. I turned to look behind us and frowned at the scene.

"There," I whispered to Stellan, nodding, not wanting to draw too much attention to our target.

He followed my gaze, jaw tightening at what he saw.

Two twin boys danced in perfect unison to the tunes of an old elf's drum.

We squeezed our past a packed square of spectators and to the front of the crowd. White paint on brown skin and black, slicked-back hair. They wore the same outfit: brown leather trouser pants and red shirts with large silver buttons. They smiled and continued their choreographed dance and bowed once the music stopped.

I let go of Maxim's hand and clapped. I fished a large gold coin out of my pocket.

Stellan put a hand out to stop me. "No. Don't do it."

"I know what I'm doing," I said, and tossed the coin into the basket set beside the elf.

He looked down at the coin, then lifted dull gray eyes to mine. A crocked grin came to his slim, sunken face.

I saw it then; a brief flash of black crossing before the whites of his deep-set eyes.

Yes. A corsus.

Stellan outstretched his scepter and lowered his hood, inciting a collective gasp from the assembled faeries. They bowed and stepped away, giving him room to step closer to the corsus and his minions.

"We banish you back to The Veil," Stellan said.

"Stupid children," the corsus sneered. "I've been waiting for you."

I grunted as he shed the skin of the elf and leaped into the sky. Gray as ash, with hollow eyes and red tendrils weaving through his face like tattoos. Screams of terror erupted from the crowd as the two boys also shed their skin and joined the larger corsus in the air, hovering, encased in black smoke.

What a sight that made. The crowd stopped watching, and ran in all directions.

The Wind-Walkers looked to Stellan and I.

"Your royal highness," the captain said. "We have no power over this evil."

Stellan nodded. "I know. That's why Maxim and I were born."

The corsus hissed, and the three of them blew something into the air. With the waving of his scepter, Stellan cracked the ground, and made ice shoot into the sky.

The pointed end impaled one of the minions, his cry echoing off the stone buildings that stood in either corner.

Still, black dust hit my face and seeped into my eyes, nose, and mouth.

I struggled to breathe, falling backward onto the ground.

"Maxim," Stellan called. "Don't breathe it in!"

"Its too late," I shouted, clutching my throat as the burning dusk ripped through my throat and into my lungs.

I could no longer see. All I heard were the sounds of a battle, and the pained yells of the corsus.

My entire body pricked all over, like all of the blood within would burst from my pores. The black dust found its ways into my blood stream. A fiery torment burned me from the inside out, and I wanted to die.

"Glory be mine," the corsus cried, and darkness took over, pinning me down until I lost all senses and succumbed.

CHAPTER 5

The Aether

The road from the Crimson Tower was one of darkness and uneven terrain. A pale moon lit the forest on either side and the worn path the carriage took.

"Here," Queen Sorcha said. "Drink some more."

She handed me another metal flask of warm brunberry elixir, something she had brewed before venturing across the borders from Allandria.

I accepted and drank enough the quench my thirst and the nagging hunger that ate away at my stomach. It was supposed to give me vitality. Though the taste of licorice lingered on my tongue, I was still waiting to feel such an effect.

We'd been traveling for hours, and Queen Sorcha sat across from me as I snuggled against Kala and fought dozing. It was cold, even with the heavy cloak she'd given me pressed tightly against my body. I was used to being uncomfortable and dreaming of warm baths like I'd gotten each night as a child.

It was good that I had experienced a better life—a normal one —but it made me realize just how spoiled I'd been. I was a princess, though my family and I were exiled, we lived a life of luxury. The privilege of a bath was a foreign concept to me now. I'd gotten used to scrubbing myself with rough cloths in frigid water.

As Queen Sorcha studied me with those ethereal emerald eyes of hers, I was never more self-conscious of the stench that rose from my body in the midst of such a delicate and composed creature such as her. While she smelled of mint oil, I couldn't ignore the aroma of layers of sweat and dirt that rose from my rags.

"You'll soon be returned to your former splendor, Princess. You'll shine like a new golden coin."

I lifted a brow. Had she been reading my thoughts? I hoped not. I wasn't exactly sure what faeries from the Seelie Court could do.

The thought of her reading my mind left me wary. Throughout the ride, I'd gone from thoughts of escaping the carriage to find a quiet place to live out the rest of my life with Kala, to accepting my fate.

After so many years in prison, I began to wonder if I was truly fit to be a princess, or a queen for that matter. I was a stranger to the customs I should have learned while I was a prisoner. My grandmother had done all she could to prepare me, but I couldn't help sensing I had no idea what I was getting myself into.

Then, again, there was something innate inside of me that begged to be satisfied. The Guardians had blessed me when I was born. They'd bestowed an ancient power and divine calling that I couldn't ignore. I wasn't the only one given the gift.

The other elements called out to me from different corners of the world, and for years I'd had to close my eyes and suppress my yearning to be united with them.

"Thank you," I said, swallowing against the dryness in my throat. I took another sip of the elixir. "For taking me from that wretched place. I was starting to think I'd die there. Every day, I waited for the warden to open the door and march me out to the gallows."

"It was the least I could do. After years of war with the humans, I requested the honor of freeing you myself."

"So, you aren't afraid of me?"

"Of course, not," she said with a chuckle. "Why would I fear you?"

Shrugging, I looked to Kala who was sleeping, her head rested on my lap as her body took up nearly the entire seat.

"Being from the Unseelie Court usually elicits prejudice from your court. We're all tricksters and evil creatures, apparently."

She shook her head with a sigh. "That's nonsense. I've lived a very long time, and I know that many facts have been bent to fit the perception some faeries would like to define the Unseelie. No. We were all one in the beginning. The fact that you come from the land of dark magic is actually *why* you were chosen.

The Seelie and Unseelie Court have been at odds for centuries, just like the humans. But, I think its time we stop dividing ourselves. The future demands unity."

Interesting. I still couldn't help but worry about what the faeries of Allandria would think of me.

"Did you fight?" I asked. "In the war?"

"Oh no," she said, smoothing her emerald skirt. "Of course, not. I don't use a sword. Well, I guess you can say I fight with my intellect. I've been making policies and negotiating treaties. Finally, King Aerion and the other four kings agreed to one. So, for the first time in nearly a century, the magic-born will have peace with the humans."

I sat up a little taller. "Why? What made them agree to peace?"

She tilted her head. "Because you and the other Elementals will put the world right again. The Veil between the living and the dead needs to be repaired. Emperor Jasper stalks the realms, causing pain and discord. Only you and the Elementals can stop him."

Such a revelation stunned me into silence. It made sense. They needed me to reverse the damage my ancestors had done after centuries of power struggles and war.

"So, I'm not free at all it seems."

"Of course, you are," she assured me. "You will rule all of the magic-born. Just wait and see."

We settled into a quiet that left me alone with my thoughts.

Queen Sorcha yawned and opened a small book. How she could read in the dark was a mystery, but I kept my mouth shut as her eyes scanned whatever was written on the cream parchment.

The sound of the steady trot of the horses as they pulled us along lulled me in and out of sleep. It wasn't until they made a sudden stop that I fully awakened.

"That's odd," she said, leaning over to look out the carriage window, and my teeth chattered as an icy wind swept inside. "Harold, why have we stopped?"

When Harold didn't respond, I tensed. Something wasn't right. The horses made a strange neighing sound as if they were being strangled. Sitting up in my seat, I followed her gaze out the window to see dancing flames coming closer and closer to us from the dark forest outside.

Humans. My eyes widened as I realized that several armed men were approaching.

It wasn't until one of the lights came soaring toward us that Queen Sorcha shared my fear.

I knew my freedom wasn't meant to last long. They'd come to kill me.

CHAPTER 6

K ala growled, standing on all fours, ready to pounce.
"Shall I handle this?" Kala asked, lifting her glowing eyes to the queen's.

Dark figures emerged and I realized that outside the carriage was a mob of people with torches, spears, and swords.

Queen Sorcha held up a hand. "No, your immanence. I can handle it."

"They're blocking the path," I said.

"Bloody fools," Queen Sorcha said. "I swear they never learn."

"Can't we go around?" I asked, my pulse quickening as the carriage began to rock from their pushing.

They began chanting so loudly that I had to resist the urge to cover my ears. Such anger and hate. I was used to being hated, but nothing like this. The prison guards never shouted insults and slurs.

"Hand over the witch."

Witch?

"Give us the witch."

"She is not welcome in Tythra or anywhere else in the human realm."

I paled, an icy ripple racing up my spine. They were talking about me.

"We are leaving, actually," Queen Sorcha assured them.

A large hand reached in and tried to open the locked carriage door. Queen Sorcha pointed her wand at him and sent a shard of red light into his palm, zapping him. The man snatched his hand back with a howl.

Visions of my mother and father being ripped away from me as I screamed and cried returned. If my grandmother hadn't held me back, I would have clung to my father's leg and been carried off to the gallows along with them.

"Don't they know you're their only chance at being free from those blasted dark sprites?"

Panicked, I looked from her and to the fire that began to rise. We were going to die, and she was acting as if they were simply coming over for a little spat. No, I knew better.

Closing my eyes, I began to call on the power I'd been awaiting all of my life. It had to present itself now.

"No," she said. "Don't shift. Not now. You must save your strength."

My eyes popped open and my jaw hung. "You *are* reading my mind, aren't you?"

With a shrug, she frowned at the men outside. She pulled a band off of a rolled scroll and held it up to the window.

"I have a royal decree here from the king. Now, step aside so we can pass. We don't want any trouble."

For a moment, there was a tense silence. A few hushed whispers passed between the burly men outside and the cloaked holy men with them.

I couldn't help but hold my breath as we awaited their reply. With narrowed eyes, I examined the golden embroidery on the black cloaks worn by the clerics outside. Black eyes looked back at me, and I coiled back with realization.

I'd seen those symbols before. The men who had taken my parents away had worn them on their cloaks.

How many times had I had nightmares of the clerics and soldiers coming in the night to rip me from my meager cot in the Crimson Tower and carrying me to my death?

"See?" Queen Sorcha asked through clenched teeth. "It's all here, in writing."

The carriage shook as a torch came crashing into the side, sending flames flying.

There was our answer.

She shook her head, more annoyed than afraid, and took a wand from a holster strapped and buckled around her shoulder and waist. She tapped it twice to the wooden door and it lit up a bright red. With a glance at me, she nodded to the mob of shouting humans outside.

"Hold open the curtain, my dear."

I did as I was told and hurried to hold the maroon curtains open.

Her eyes turned completely white. She lifted her wand and with a mumbled series of words I'd never heard, a bright light shot forth from the tip of the wand. Then, a translucent sphere of air appeared before us, spinning, and gathering energy.

My eyes widened as the sphere grew until it seeped out of the carriage and enveloped the entire thing.

The shouts and curses from outside were muted and Queen Sorcha pointed her wand directly at the mob.

"Well," she said. "That'll be enough of that."

I sat on the edge of my seat and watched in awe as the carriage was lifted into the sky. I held onto the window ledge as we ascended high into the clouds.

"How did you do that?" My jaw hung as I looked down at the dark thatch of forest and how it ended at an expansive meadow littered with white trees encrusted with snow. It was beautiful, like lights in the shadows.

She sat back in her seat and rubbed her temples.

"It's nothing really, dear. Just a bit of air mixed with magic. Too bad, though. I was saving my energy for at least until we were out of Tythra. Now, I'll need to rest."

"Or course," I said as she lay down across the seat. "Will the carriage continue to fly?"

"Yes. It'll take us to the frozen sea where the Royal Guard and Prince Ewan will be waiting for us—as negotiated with King Aerion. They'll make sure we have safe passage through The Veil of the dead."

"Prince Ewan?"

She nodded, studying my face again. "Yes. The air elemental."

Stunned, I slumped back in my seat. Just brilliant. No one told me I'd meet another elemental so soon. I breathed in and tried to calm myself.

It seemed I was in for a bit of an adventure.

CHAPTER 7

The Earth Prince

"Drink," someone urged me.

At least my ears are working well. The idea didn't sound too bad. My throat was dry beyond words and ached with thirst. I didn't hesitate to part my lips.

A thick, warm, substance seeped onto my tongue and I began to cough raggedly at the saltiness.

My eyes snapped open. They met the deep-set gray gaze of the faerie who sat beside me with a wooden bowl in hand.

"Where am I? What happened?"

She placed a hand on my chest, shushing me. "Calm yourself, your highness," she said, her voice smooth and soothing.

I nodded, and rested my head on the soft, down pillow.

"Who are you? Where is Stellan?"

"Makya. Prince Stellan is waiting for you to heal. I made him go to bed," she said. "He cares for you. He sat in that chair for two days just to make sure no one harmed you while you rested."

"He did?"

"Yes. Now drink before it gets too cold."

That was surprising. Stellan liked to pretend that he was hard-ened, and uncaring. Still, we both treated each other like brothers, and brothers were often rivals.

There was a white tattoo of a bird on the right side of Makya's light brown cheek. Her hair was long and white, and though most faeries were ageless, I could tell she was an elder.

"How long have I been out?"

She reached the bowl to my mouth again. "Four days. It was quite a challenge ridding you of the corsus poison. But, I'm confi-dent that most is out of your system and you'll be free of it all within another day or two. For now, this brew will heal your aching stomach and soothe your parched throat."

"Four days," I said, grabbing a handful of my hair and staring at the ceiling. "We were supposed to leave for Allandria."

"Allandria will still be there when you recover."

"Queen Sorcha will not be pleased," I said with a heavy sigh.

"She will be glad that you are still alive, young prince. Now, do not worry yourself. Rest. Get well."

I wanted to ask more questions, but the brew lulled me into sweet sleep. Tired of the empty void, the darkness, I tried to fight it.

"*I can help you,*" a disembodied voice whispered from within.

My eyes popped open. The dim light from a single candle welcomed me.

What was that voice?

My head lolled to the side as I watched the flame flicker and dance. I heard soft singing come from the next room. The flame seemed to sway with the soft melody.

I tried to sit up, but the pain forced me back down.

The room was small, with four stone walls, and a tiny window at the top, right above the bed I lay upon.

I thought back to what had happened and vaguely remembered the corsus and his minions. Oh yes, he'd infected me with black dust. The pain was there somewhere, but manageable.

Makya was gone, and I found myself wishing she was there. There was safety in her presence. Though alone, the tiny hairs on my arms rose as the heavy gaze of another made me shoot up in bed.

A memory of a soft unnatural voice still haunted me.

A tiny cackle set me on edge.

"Who is there?" My voice came out cracked and I swallowed against the dryness. Still, I kept my eyes open wide, and refused to blink. I wanted to catch whatever was in that room with me.

My eyes shot to the candle's flame. It no longer swayed. Now it stood still, and reached higher into the air.

"*Maxim,*" the voice whispered.

Cold flooded my veins.

"Who are you?"

The flame cast a glow on the wall, and that's when I saw it; a shadow that wasn't my own, huddled in the corner.

"*Call me star, for I am as old as the universe, and have watched it shift and evolve,*" it said.

"Star?" I repeated, wetting my lips. "What do you want from me?"

"*Oh, I think you know,*" Star said. "*Emperor Jasper wants the Aether, and you will take me to her.*"

The candle flickered out and a black blanket of darkness smothered me.

CHAPTER 8

The Aether

The carriage flew for a day and a half, and landed at the edge of an icy tundra. From above, I could see into the frozen sea. Patches of dark water and slush gave way to the white shore that stretched for miles upon miles into the distance.

Queen Sorcha sighed and shook her head as we waited for Harold to open the door.

When the carriage doors were opened, snow flurries attacked us. The chill shocked my skin once the first snow flake landed on the tip of my nose. Still, more flakes flew onto my face, dusting me until the door was covered in the powder.

Harold's black beard was covered in snow, and his dark eyes glanced at me before quickly looking away.

It was then that I noticed that he was neither human nor faerie. The horns curling from his forehead were indicative of a feren, a creature from the north of Ever Frost where the giants dwelled. The bitter air didn't seem to bother him. On the contrary, it was said that the cold only made them stronger.

Still, he didn't speak. He simply stepped aside and made way for Queen Sorcha as she left the carriage and stood on the icy ground.

I was a wary. Though I'd changed into traveling clothes in the back of the carriage, I wasn't ready to endure the storm raging outside.

In leather pants more supple than any material I could recall wearing, and a cream-colored tunic with a belt and my heavy cloak and boots, I prepared myself and leaped down with a crunch of ice.

Kala followed suit and stood beside me, her eyes gazing at the dull, gray sky, and then to the outstretched frozen sea before us. It was different from what I'd imagined. The sea was frozen in some spots but a slushy consistency in others. Green and blue lights danced across the sky just above the sea. It was magical to behold, but I knew what lay ahead.

The Veil between the living and the dead. I shuddered at the thought that in just moments we'd be crossing that invisible boundary.

At the edge was a narrow black ship, with several men on deck and on shore. Though slim, it was tall, with the royal crest of Allandria on its black sails. A white dragon curled around a sword.

The Royal Guard. I swallowed and tried to get a better look. They were too far to truly make out any details, but I was looking for someone in particular.

Prince Ewan.

I'd heard his call many times. It was like an itch in my chest that I couldn't scratch. His power reached out to mine and some nights I'd weep with frustration that I couldn't reach back.

The Crimson Tower was enchanted. It muted my power and left me defenseless. Now, I was free.

"Just a short walk," Queen Sorcha said, lowering the hood of her cloak over her vibrant red hair. "And, off we go."

I did the same, pulling my hood down and tightening it at my throat. It worked at shielding myself from the tiny particles of ice that blowed at my face.

Harold unhooked the horses from the carriage and led them to us.

"You can ride with me," she said as Harold helped her up into the saddle.

I continued to search for Ewan even as I hopped onto the back of the horse behind her. I wrapped my arms around her tiny waist and held tight, still with my eyes fixed on the men in the horizon.

The thumping of my heart in my chest was so loud that I could barely hear the howling of the wind and crunch of snow as we began a slow trot away from the carriage.

Every moment that we drew closer to the ship was agonizing. I could feel his heat and smell him before I even got a look at his face. I wondered what he would look like. Would he be as handsome as I'd dreamed? In my mind, each elemental was a perfect representation of what I deemed attractive.

Bright green eyes. Taller than most of the soldiers behind him with broad shoulders and a square jaw. Black hair with hints of silver at his temples.

I realized I didn't have much to go on. I hadn't seen many men in my life. Just the guards at the tower and they all had a sullen, dirty look about them.

Under guard, Kala and I were allowed to walk the outer gardens of the tower twice a day, and occasionally I would catch a glimpse of the other prisoners. They were always kept away from me, in another area, but I would spy on them from time to time, astride Kala's back and peering over the walls of shrubbery.

No one ever seemed particularly pleasing to the eye, and no one ever spoke to me. Even the prisoners were afraid to fraternize with a witch.

Eagles soared above, searching for food, and finding nothing but white as far as the eye could see. I looked over my shoulder and caught the faintest of a glimpse of the dark forest we'd left behind.

A shriek escaped my lips as a blast of heat filled my core and rippled through my entire body. My jaw dropped and Queen Sorcha glanced back at me.

"Well, looks like Prince Ewan is excited to see you."

Prince Ewan manipulated the storm-wind, for me. It lifted my hair and brushed my face, gently, almost as if he touched me with his own hands. It was then that I realized I had no idea what I was getting myself into, but couldn't wait to find out.

White trails of powdery snow coiled and danced along the wind in an unnatural display.

Magic.

I sat up tall and looked down at my gloved hands. Even through the leather, I could see that they were glowing, as was the rest of my body. A smile came to my face, and I touched my cheek. I hadn't expected to actually be excited about meeting a stranger.

Excitement was an understatement.

CHAPTER 9

Tythra suffered an eternal night after the split of The Veil, and as we approached the camp of soldiers, my heart was in my throat. Though the anticipation made my hands sweat despite the frigid wind, I was more ready than ever.

With the dancing colors in the sky, it lit the path for us across the ice and hard-packed snow. In the horizon, I could see mountains, far, far away.

Tiny red flies buzzed around us with translucent wings. Their sudden burst of color was stark against the gray atmosphere around us.

"Disgusting little blood suckers," she hissed, swiping her hand at one as she stopped her horse just behind Harold. "Of course, they're hunting so close to The Veil. Try not to let them bite you, dear."

She lifted her hood. Snow flew from the thick wool and curled along the swift wind as she kicked her legs over the side of the horse to dismount.

I would have asked what they were, but my eyes were locked on the camp the Royal Guard had made on the icy shore.

Canvas tents lined the beach and several fires blazed high, sending orange embers into the dark sky. They wore leather and fur over their emerald armor, and all turned to behold our arrival.

Every man kneeled to her—except for one—who didn't bow as deep or linger as long. He was much different than I'd imagined, bright ice-blue eyes on the verge of being completely white lifted to mine from under long silver hair streaked faintly with a black undertone that matched his brows.

It was him.

Ewan—the wind element—one of the princes in my future court.

"We camp for the night," she said to me. "And continue the journey in the morning."

Nodding, I barely heard a word she said as the prince walked directly to me and held out a hand. I almost forgot anyone else was there, though they watched us with apt attention.

"Evening," he said in a thick accent that made my spine tingle. "Prince Ewan, at your service."

Swallowing, I glanced down and for a split second hesitated when I realized he had a metal hand. My heart skipped a beat, but I kept my face free of emotion, accepted his hand, and lowered myself to the ground. I needed to know the story behind that hand, and found myself a great deal more curious than I thought I'd be.

He was tall, almost a full foot taller—another characteristic I was correct in assuming. I noticed a point to his ears and was pleasantly surprised. He was an elf.

"We finally meet."

Nodding, I prayed he couldn't hear how loudly my heart beat against my ribs. The fact that he was technically the first man I'd met who wasn't a prison guard left my throat dry and my cheeks hot.

For a moment, I could breathe again as he took his heavy gaze from my face and turned to Queen Sorcha.

"Queen Mother, there have been reports of elves in the territory just beyond The Veil."

She folded her hands before her and pursed her lips. "They're your people, Prince Ewan. What are they doing there?"

"Well, they're from a lesser kingdom to the west, but I gather they are seeking refuge."

"From what, exactly?"

He shrugged. "Civil war, probably. The report didn't say."

After a long sigh, she nodded. "Very well. I'll deal with it once we get through The Veil. Any reports of weyrs?"

Prince Ewan shook his head. "No. The wind says we should be safe if we go at first light."

"We will be ready," she said, clasping a hand onto his shoulder. "I will retire to my tent and get some rest. You two should do the same."

She kissed me on the cheek. "Sleep well," she said and headed to one of the larger tents set up for her.

Once she was gone, the silence between Ewan and I was filled with the faint howling of the wind.

"Do you know how long I've waited to be alone with you? I would have destroyed armies and climbed the Crimson Tower to rescue you if Queen Sorcha would have let me."

Kala sat beside me, watching him.

"A dire wolf," he said, smiling down at her.

"A changeling," Kala corrected, surprising him as she shifted and stood before us in an indigo gown and gray cloak. Long white hair fell to her lower back and gently swayed. Faint wrinkles creased at the corners of her thin eyes, yet she looked no older than a faerie of forty despite living at least a century.

He stumbled backward, eyes widened. "Blessed spirits."

She stretched and rolled her neck before resting a critical gaze at the prince. "Blessed spirits, indeed."

A faint smile came to my lips. "Prince Ewan," I said. "Meet my grandmother, Dowager Queen Kala of Mordigan."

He raked a hand through his silky hair, and looked from my grandmother to me in awe. "Bloody brilliant."

Kala pulled her cloak closer and looked down her narrow nose at him with ice-blue eyes. "You didn't think the Queen Mother would leave you two alone, did you?"

For the first time since the queen saved me from the Crimson Tower, I was at ease. Even though we were camped on the beach outside of The Veil that separated the living from the dead, having my grandmother there in her faerie form brought me solace.

I covered my giggle with my hands. I wasn't entirely alone during my imprisonment. Kala would always find a way to visit. Whether it was as a butterfly flying into my window, or a dove, she was one of the most rare of fairies. I was lucky to have her.

Eleven years in the Crimson Tower would have been unbearable without her company. When she was with me, my days would be filled with tutoring, etiquette lessons, and the occasional story about my parents and how they met at the Harvest Ball.

Though it took a great deal of energy and power to shift, she was allowed to return to her faerie form on occasion, if only for a little while.

My grandmother's existence was lengthened because of her ability and each time she returned to that of a faerie, it shaved precious years off her life.

"Of course," he said, clearing his throat. "I simply wanted to—"

"Yes, yes," she said, cutting him off. "Show us to our tent, young man. The princess needs to rest. You can charm her as much as you'd like in the morning."

Prince Ewan bowed to her and turned to obey her command.

"As you wish, Dowager Queen."

CHAPTER 10

We followed him from the horses and through the tight-knit arrangement of tents and huddled soldiers warming themselves around fires with embers that sparked and crackled in the air.

As we walked by, the soldiers bowed their heads to the prince and cast their curious stares my way.

While intimidated, I knew that this was just the beginning. Even dressed in traveler's clothes, I stood out amongst them. A dark faerie hadn't been welcomed by the light since the split of Rune in the First Age.

Prince Ewan led us to the tent we would stay in for the night. The whispers and stares from the soldiers reminded me of just how different life would be once we crossed over to the magic realm. I was used to being beheld with disgust, hatred, and fear.

These men—adored me. They even addressed me as your majesty.

I nodded to them, as grandmother had trained me to do. She'd done her best to prepare me for what was ahead, but I worried that there was nothing that would calm the butterflies fluttering in my belly.

We crunched along the icy shore, and Prince Ewan stopped just outside one of the larger tents made of canvas.

"Here we are," he said, turning to me. "Wait until you see your private apartment in the palace."

"Thank you, Prince Ewan," Kala said.

We shared a look as he held the cloth door open for her.

A brief scent of burning coals wafted out of the tent, and I shuddered, eager to warm myself before a fire.

Once she was out of sight, he took my hands and brought my knuckles to his lips. They were cold and dry from the weather, but still sent heat up my arms to my face.

"I look forward to the morning when we can learn more about one another," he said. "I have waited all of my life to meet you, and even though we have an eternity together, I simply can't hold back my excitement."

I smiled. "Neither can I."

"Its been ten years since you've seen a proper sunrise, I gather," Prince Ewan said.

Nodding, I looked to the sky. "I am quite eager to see one."

"Allandria Castle is set in the center of the kingdom, but the towers stand tall and can see the countryside for miles. I'll take you to my favorite place to see the sunrise and set once we arrive and get settled."

"Do you miss your home?" I asked, stalling. I wasn't quite ready to say goodbye. We'd just met and there was so much I wanted to learn about him and where he came from. "Back in Ostrum?"

"Not really," he said. "Ostrum isn't nearly as opulent as Allandria."

"And, your family?"

"Ah, well. My father probably barely notices that I'm gone. My mother passed when I was a child."

"Oh, dear. I'm sorry to hear it." Even though he'd mentioned the death of his mother, he still had it in him to smile at me, though I detected a hint of bitterness in his voice.

Shrugging, he looked ahead. "Nothing to apologize for, princess. It is life, isn't it? I'm afraid I only have traces of immortal blood on my father's side. Poor Mother caught ill when the plague came in from the merchant ships sailing from human territory."

"Kala mentioned that," I said. "It killed thousands."

He snorted. "Probably more than that. Bloody humans and their diseases. Wait, your grandmother let's you call her by her given name?"

I shrugged. "She's always insisted."

"Celeste," Kala called. "It's getting late."

Blushing, I flickered my eyes up to his and sighed. "I suppose I should sleep now."

"Yes. I suppose so," he said, taking my hands into his. "You're more beautiful than I could have ever dreamed." He brushed my hair from my face before kissing my forehead.

Kala cleared her throat and he chuckled. I shrugged and held back another giggle of my own.

We were betrothed, but there were limits to what physical contact was appropriate until we were officially wed.

My cheeks heated at the thought of what would be allowed afterward, and reddened as I realized I was betrothed to two others whom I hadn't even met yet. I hoped this grand plan the Guardians had devised would work.

"Good night, princess," he said, with a slight bow, and left me to my rest.

I watched him stalk off into the dark camp and glanced at the pale moon. All of my life I'd suffered. Could it truly be my time for a reward for all that I'd been forced to endure?

Inside, Kala had shifted back into a dire wolf. She rested on the floor of the tent next to a stone pit filled with hot coals. "It's too cold to be a faerie on this night," she said. "Won't you shed your faerie form and join me?"

Sighing, I removed my cloak and settled onto the bed made for me on the floor. Wool and down padding was only a step better than what I'd slept on in prison. "You know I cannot shift," I said.

She lowered her head to her paws and closed her eyes. "You will," she said. "Give it time."

As I pulled the covers over my body and head, I contemplated all that had occurred and what was to come. The Veil was all that stood in between me and the realm I would soon rule.

"Are we sure about all of this?"

"It is your destiny," Kala said. "It's what you were born for."

"But," I pursed my lips and reconsidered what I was about to ask. We didn't talk about the darkness hovering above my head, but I needed to know. "What about the Unseelie?"

"Enough worrying, Celeste. They can't touch us once we are in Allandria. Forget them."

Closing my eyes, I drifted into a feverish slumber that reminded me that not everyone in the magic realm would be pleased with my return.

No, my very own tribe wanted me dead more than the humans. More than anyone.

CHAPTER 11

The Air Prince

I stood outside her tent for a moment, utterly amazed by her. Running a hand through my hair, I looked to the sky and thanked the Guardians for choosing me to be part of her court.

I'd felt her presence since I was a boy, and waited patiently for when we would meet.

Still, nothing could have prepared me for her beauty, poise, or the fact that her grandmother was a wolf.

Chuckling to myself, I left to join the soldiers around the fire. Sleep was something that didn't come naturally to me. It was an elusive concept that always seemed to runaway whenever I chased it.

You don't sleep peacefully after you've seen the things I'd seen. Elves were ruthless. Everyone knew that. Sons were a blessing to any queen and king, but seven were a nightmare.

The rivalries and political intrigue was utterly exhausting. I was glad to leave my kingdom and fight in the war.

Now that it was over, another was just beginning. My smile

faded at that thought. I crossed the camp and stopped at a circle of soldiers seated around a crackling fire. I began to sit when Queen Sorcha approached from the darkness.

"Prince Ewan," she said.

I lifted a brow.

"A word in private."

I nodded and followed, swallowing a lump in my throat. The steel in her eyes made my blood run cold, and as she lead me into the darkness from whence she came, I rested the palm of my hand on the hilt of my sword.

Paranoia was a constant fuel. You don't grow up around six ruthless young men all plotting to take your spot without becoming painfully aware of the intentions of others.

Queen Sorcha had summoned me. She was the one to bring the Elementals together. Still, one could never truly know who to trust.

My jaw tightened as she led me away from the camp, away from the ears or eyes of anyone else.

Under the dancing colors of the night sky, she faced me, her pale skin illuminated by the light of the moon.

"What do you think of her?" Queen Sorcha asked, her voice bland, showing no emotion.

"She's stunning."

"Of course, she's beautiful. But, what else?"

I shrugged. "I've barely had a chance to speak with her. Is something wrong?"

Frustration marred her face as she rubbed her hands together. "The fire prince will not come. He refuses to be bound in eternity to her."

My jaw dropped. "How can that be? The Guardians chose him the same way they chose the rest of us. Lancel is a hot-head, but he is no fool. He cannot shirk his duty."

"Don't you think I know? Everything will be ruined if Prince Lancel doesn't heed the calling."

"Surely, Stellan and Maxim will come?"

She nodded. "They are two of the most dutiful young men I've ever met, besides yourself, of course. They will be in Allandria when we arrive. But, we need all of you for the magic to work."

I folded my arms across my chest. For the first time since the field of battle, true fear filled my heart like an icicle stabbed into my chest.

None of the other knew Emperor Jasper like I did. I glanced down at my metal arm. Nor did they feel the true measure of his wrath.

CHAPTER 12

The Earth Prince

"Now, this is the final test to make sure you are properly healed," Makya said in her soft and reassuring voice.

I nodded, swallowing. "Very well," I said, mustering my courage. "I trust you."

She smiled at me. "Thank you," she said, and touched my cheek with the back of her hand, then my heart.

"Anything?" I asked, anxious for the answer.

"Nothing yet."

She pulled a jar from the table at my side and stuck in hands inside. Then, she took them out of the jar and smeared white dust onto my entire, naked body.

I held my breath, not entirely sure what to expect as she studied the dust and how it began to crawl across my body.

This had to work.

They'd never let me leave Ever Frost and travel to Allandria if Star still infected my body.

Tense, and with a heart racing faster than the race horses back in Kyushu, I prayed to the Guardians. Then, something stirred. I clenched my fists as the white dust began to burn into me, seeping below my skin, into muscle, and bones.

A pained grunt escaped my lips. Covered in sweat, I leaned forward for a better look, and she placed a hand against my forehead and pushed me back down.

"Stay still, dear prince," she whispered, a finger held to her lips. "Let me handle the rest."

Then, she lifted from the chair by her flapping wings and flew over me as if searching for something.

When her eyes widened, I froze in terror. Almost too afraid to speak, my throat closed.

"What is it?" I asked from between clenched teeth.

A jolt from inside rocked my body and I threw my head back onto the bed.

She held me down, and as I looked into her eyes, I saw such concern that I knew I might die on this day.

"Hold still," she said. "This may hurt."

With that, my gut wretched and convulsed as something foreign—something unnatural crawled up my chest and to my throat.

"Open your mouth," she demanded.

I obeyed, tears burning my eyes.

I gagged and to my utter shock, a black, snake-like creature peeked its head out of my mouth. Slippery, and covered in my blood, it turned a golden eye my way.

That—was living inside of me?

A scream vibrated against my throat, and Makya pulled it by its head with all of her might.

It squealed and fought, but the elder faerie was stronger and ripped it free from my body.

The force of the fight sent her flying backward and crashing to the floor, the creature still locked in her grasp.

Gasping for breath, she held the creature into the air, triumphant.

She glanced at me with a smile on her face. "We got it," she cheered, and tossed it into the flames of the fire that burned and crackled in the hearth.

Relieved, I slumped back onto the bed in a pool of sweat and blood.

CHAPTER 13

The Aether

Nightmares of the Unseelie Court lingered in the back of my head once I awakened and prepared for the journey between realms.

Though it was true that the dark faeries of Rune weren't as terrifying as the creatures of The Veil, it did not lessen my fear of them.

Sprites, imps, corsus, and weyrs didn't haunt my dreams. The faeries who forced my family from our home did.

The fact that they exiled my family for wanting to unite with the Seelie Court worried me. My return would not be well received. I was from the Unseelie Court, and I was about to do the one thing they despised.

Kala stood watch outside of the tent as I scrubbed my face with a rag soaked in hot water. I still felt filthy, and the prospect of a warm bath made me even more eager to reach the palace as soon as possible.

I raked my fingers through golden tangles and pulled my hair into a knot at the back of my head. Dressed in the tunic and pants

Queen Sorcha had given me, I pulled on my fur-lined cloak and boots and went out into the bitter cold.

Prince Ewan stood before my grandmother in her wolf form.

Her white fur rustled in the wind as she eyed him, unblinking, making him visibly uncomfortable.

He was as handsome as the night before, dressed warmly in heavy furs and leather. His hood was up; his long black hair pulled back. Still, wild strands flew free and crossed his face as he smirked at me.

"Morning, princess." With his hand on the pommel of the sword at his side, he was the picture of a dashing knight, ready for battle.

My hands tingled. I yearned for a sword.

Amongst the many secret training my grandmother gave me during my imprisonment, the use of a sword was one of my favorites.

Queen Sorcha chose to fight with her wit and intellect. I, on the other hand, preferred a sharp blade.

"Morning," I repeated, though it was still so dark one wouldn't know the difference between day and night in this part of the world.

"Did you sleep well?"

"Yes," I lied.

I'd barely slept at all. The nightmares of fairies with purple hair, and glittering eyes had kept me up most of the night. They'd threatened to destroy us if we ever returned, and here I was —returning.

"Lovely, let's get a move on then, shall we? You only stand face to face with weyrs once in your life, right? Well, this would be my second time."

Nervous, I accepted his hand and he tucked it into the small of his elbow and led me to the ship. The mention of weyrs caught me off guard.

"Do you truly think we will see any?"

"No, I was just fooling with you. I didn't see any on my way across the first time. We'll be fine."

Something told me not to completely trust those words. I knew more than anyone that things rarely went the way you expected them to.

Kala had told me that the war probably wouldn't last more than a year. I stopped hoping after five passed by without any word.

"Just keep your eyes and ears open, and stick with me. I won't let anything happen to you," he said, which calmed me, if only for a moment.

The frozen sea worried me. I'd seen it from the sky and knew that below the thick ice were dark depths that I didn't care to explore. I held onto him, tightly and gingerly stepped across the slick ice. Each step was a risk, but we managed to make our way across the solid portion and to the ship.

Prince Ewan gave me a lift to climb the rope ladder that led up onto deck.

My eyes kept glancing down at the slush that gathered at the base of the ship and the dark water lapping at it.

"Celeste, my dear," Queen Sorcha said, reaching out her hands toward me once I was safely on deck.

Her red hair was braided that morning, a stark contrast to her black hood.

"Come. I want to give you something."

Prince Ewan fell into step beside me as we crossed the slick deck. The soldiers and ship crew prepared for our departure, shouting orders and pulling ropes for the sail. They scrubbed the deck of any remaining ice and barely gave me more than a second glance.

My eyes were cast toward the shimmering film stretched ahead of us. Every so often, you could see a flicker of light and the movement of the air like smoke or a mist rising from the sea. The Veil was mostly invisible, but it had a distinctive feel to it. The air grew tight as we crossed the boundary and entered the realm of the dead. Nothing changed, visually, but the pressure made my head feel as though it would explode.

I couldn't see anything, but, I sensed eyes on me. The presence of a few forgotten—and perhaps curious—spirits lingering this close to the human realm made my skin crawl with dread.

Thank the Guardians I wasn't given the power to see the spirits, or I would have kept my eyes closed and hoped for the best that we'd make it out alive.

Queen Sorcha sat on a bench and motioned for us to join her on either side.

I sat down and felt the cold on my bottom. Crossing my legs and wrapping my arms around myself, I caught a glimpse of something right before me. I jumped. The tiny hairs inside my ears tickled me and the air grew thick.

"Did you see that?"

"I did. Just ignore it," Queen Sorcha said. "All it wants is attention."

Another flicker of light danced across my eyes and I coiled back as a translucent figure flashed before me. "What is it?"

"A pixie spirit. No need to worry. They are curious, but harmless," she said.

Pursing my lips, I tried to ignore the constant attempts to get my attention as Queen Sorcha pulled two medallions from a pouch. It was small, with a heart shaped face and cold, black eyes and silver wings.

What's your name?

I tensed when it's faint voice permeated into my brain.

I can keep a secret. Tell me your name.

I shuddered.

"Here," Queen Sorcha said, and I had to turn away from the spirit to get it to leave me alone. "This is your official Allandrian charms. Keep it with you at all times and you'll be protected from any dark spirits or weyrs that might be lurking about."

I snatched mine from her hand and pulled the chain over my head and around my neck.

Prince Ewan chuckled and pulled his from under his shirt. "I'll be keeping mine on even when we are free of The Veil."

My cheeks reddened. "Pardon my manners," I mumbled. "Thank you." I was just grateful to have something to ward off any evil.

She patted my hand and stood. "Of course, dear. Now, we should arrive in Allandria within a day or two."

I lifted a brow. "It's that close?"

"Indeed. But, Allandria is vast and covers much of faerie territory. You'll soon see."

She stood and cracked her delicate little knuckles.

Kala flew onto the ship in the form of an eagle and shifted back into her wolf-form before our eyes.

"To admit that I am terribly jealous of your abilities would be a bit of an understatement," Queen Sorcha said.

Kala tilted her head upward. "It does have its advantages. Without my gift, I wouldn't have survived the takeover of Mordigan by that fiend and her army."

"Yes. You have been blessed, Dowager Queen," Queen Sorcha said, nodding.

"One day, Celeste will have the ability to shift as well."

The queen's eyes shot to mine. Her brows furrowed. "You mean, she hasn't been able to yet?"

"No. It will come, with time."

"I see," she said. "No matter. It's in her blood. I made sure of that."

Something in her eyes worried me as she looked me up and down.

I tensed and watched her walk away without another word.

"I hope I haven't disappointed her," I said to Kala.

"She will get over it," she replied, and curled at my feet. "They can't expect you to be everything at all times. You're still just a girl."

She was right. Sometimes even I forgot that. I was seventeen, and the fate of the world rested on my shoulders. It was a heavy weight for such a small girl.

Prince Ewan gave my shoulder a squeeze. "You'll come to see that Queen Sorcha simply has high standards for everyone. Prince Stellan can attest to her eagerness for perfection."

That name was familiar. Tucking a fallen strand behind my ear, I turned to him. "Who is Stellan?"

"Oh," Prince Ewan said, rubbing his chin. "He's her son."

Son? My eyes widened. *My old playmate.*

How could I forget the fun we'd had as children? Queen Sorcha had brought him along when she'd visited my parents and I. Though she'd taken a sample of my blood, the shock of it was remedied by playing with the wild, fearless little red-haired boy.

"I remember him, now," I said under my breath. "He always loved the lake behind my grandmother's estate."

He nodded. "Makes sense. He is the water element, after all."

CHAPTER 14

S tunned, I stood there mouth agape.

Water element?

Of course. Why didn't I realize that? He had shown me his power as children. The boy with the red hair had been a fond memory, until even he became a blur with all of the rest of my memories.

I looked down at my hands. A young boy had his power at the age of five. Why did mine insist on remaining dormant even as an adult?

Balling my hands into fists and lowering them to my sides, I began to wonder if I was truly the girl the Guardians had chosen. Perhaps Queen Sorcha had it all wrong.

"Kala," I said, coming down to my knees before her.

She tilted her head as I wrapped my arms around her furry neck. "What is it, Celeste?"

"I'm worried," I whispered. "What if my magic never comes? How could it be dormant for so many years?"

"I see," she said. "You worry too much. You are the Aether. You have the power to control all of the elements. It is within *you* to summon the power. When you free yourself of all fear and useless thoughts, you will be able to call it forth."

"I don't see how. We've been trying for years."

She nuzzled my neck. "Perhaps that's what you're doing wrong. Stop trying and let it come to you naturally. No one can teach you how to be an Aether. They are rare and there are never more than one in the entire world at any given time. You must look within, Celeste. I believe in you. We all do."

I sighed and pursed my lips. Why couldn't I feel it if it was truly there?

I could feel Ewan's magic, and that of the other Elementals even though we'd never met. Each individual stream of power was strong enough to wake me from sleep, or cause me to pause during any given activity.

"Try not to overexcite yourself. We still have quite a bit of traveling to do before we reach Allandria."

I nodded, and watched her walk away.

Her words lingered in my mind as I stood. *No one can teach you,* she'd said. I looked for the prince.

We shall see about that.

The ship began to set sail, slowly wading through the ice and slush. My hair—now blue with worry—blew in the wind as I joined him at the bulwark of the ship. I wrapped my hands around the rail and looked out over to the passing sea. We stood like that for quite some time, enjoying the quiet and each other's company.

Surprisingly, Kala left us to our solitude. Though, she did keep watch from afar, occasionally lifting her head to watch us stand at the other end of the ship.

He took my hands into his, and lifted them to the sky. With my palm pressed to his, he closed his eyes.

The cold metal was smooth and silky, unlike the bars of my window in the Crimson Tower.

Though the darkness of The Veil shrouded us like a thick blanket. A heavy fog rose from the water's surface and made the air humid despite the cold.

"Prince Ewan," I began, giving him a sidelong glance.

"Yes?"

"Can you teach me to use my power?"

He rubbed his chin with his metal hand, eyeing my hair as it shimmered in the moonlight. "How much do you know about the elements?"

"Everything," I said. "Kala made sure I knew as much as possible."

"Well, as the wind element, I can only try to teach you about that one."

Good. That's all I wanted. Just a try. Anything to prove I wasn't a useless fraud.

"Thank you," I said, breathing a sigh of relief. For a moment, my worries melted into the back of my mind as his eyes met mine. For years, his power had reached out to me and now we were finally together. I looked away and cleared my throat.

"Don't thank me just yet," he said with a chuckle. "I've never been much of a teacher."

He lifted his metal hand. I realized that it was made of bronze and carved with intricate symbols. The cuff ended at a leather bracer at the wrist and his shirt brushed the shiny surface.

"I didn't get this from teaching."

I forgot my manners as I reached out to touch the metal again, tracing the engravings. "How *did* you get it?"

"War," he said with a shrug, but didn't stop me. "We've been at it for years."

Guilt filled my chest and I lowered my eyes and took my hand away as if it had touched fire. "Because of me," I said in a soft voice.

"No," he said. "Not just because of you. The past decade has been a time of darkness and suffering. Many of us fought to put an end to it. Even though you are free, the fight is still going on.

The Veil is open, and with that comes all manner of creatures and evil that do not belong in our world. The war is far from over."

A bone-chilling scream snatched our attention from one another as we both spun around to see one of the soldiers being snatched away by a creature with black wings.

My lips parted and the color drained from my face as I beheld my first encounter with one of the nightmarish beings that stalked the world.

A weyr.

CHAPTER 15

Every inch of my body tensed as I watched in horror as the weyr stole the soldier from deck, wrapped its wings around the both of them and sent blood spraying into the air. At that moment, it got colder, unbearably so.

My heart thumped in my chest, and I found myself reaching for Prince Ewan's sword.

"No," he yelled over the screams as more weyrs lowered themselves down from the dark sky. He pushed me aside, and with a ring of steel, he pulled his sword free. "Stay back, Celeste. I can't have you getting hurt."

"Give me something to defend myself with, then," I shouted back. "Don't leave me cowering over here like a lost kitten."

My words must have surprised him, for he beheld me with bewilderment, before snatching a dagger from his boot and placing the hilt into my open hand.

"Very well, then," he said. "Try not to stab yourself. It's quite sharp."

I frowned at the comment, but pursed my lips and turned back to the chaos that took place on our ship. At this rate, I'd never make it to the palace alive.

Queen Sorcha emerged from below deck, her wand in hand and in her night clothes. In sheer white, her red hair stood out against her clothes and pale skin.

The soldiers assembled and abandoned their posts, swords in hand, bows ready. They were fighting for their lives as the weyrs snatched their brothers away.

Queen Sorcha took to the skies, her nightgown flourishing around her as she spun and conjured a shield around herself that the attackers couldn't penetrate.

They tried, taking their attention from the lowly soldiers and ripping at the air around her with their sharp claws, even going so far as to try to bite the shield with their fangs.

They were feral, merciless creatures, and her magic shot out at them with equal ferocity. Blue lights that zapped into their skinny frames and obliterated them.

Kala leaped into the air, taking down a weyr and ripping out its throat with her teeth.

My eyes widened. I'd never seen my grandmother be so brutal.

While I stood there marveling at the violence all around me, Prince Ewan fought alongside the soldiers, taking down winged creatures left and right, impaling them with his sword through their chests. He was fast, and efficient. Precise.

I'd never seen such skill.

While the soldiers fought with wild, hacking attacks, Prince Ewan's moves were fluid, almost like a dance. Every swing of the sword was met with bone and flesh.

Sweat beaded on my forehead and between my breasts. I was frozen. There were too many. More than a dozen darted back and forth as fast as light, but cloaked in darkness like shadows.

All of my training in the Crimson Tower meant nothing against a real threat. Kala had taught me everything she knew about how to wield a sword, and I had been confident that I could execute my training. But, this was the real world.

I was still that scared little girl, defenseless, watching as her world was ripped away from her.

A cry escaped my lips as two sharp talons dug themselves into my shoulders. The pain was shocking, and in the heat of battle, I forgot all of my training. Prince Ewan was right to doubt me.

I was utterly useless.

Prince Ewan stopped fighting and shot a look my way as I was lifted into the air and flown away.

My scream was all that was left of me as I was taken into the mist.

Into The Veil.

CHAPTER 16

Terror like no other filled my body as my scream cloaked the night, vibrating across the misty air that comprised The Veil. The yells of Prince Ewan and Queen Sorcha became hollow the more distance was put between us.

For a moment, wind had wrapped around me, but the creatures were so fast that whatever it was fizzled behind us.

The weyrs carried me far from the ship, far from my prince and the soldiers. My feet dangled and my eyes beheld the horrifying inky black below.

I was going to die. My throat ached from the hard lump in it.

Was this how it would end—with the Aether captured and killed by undead creatures?

My scream continued to rise in waves as they weaved in and out of caves and around trees. We were no longer over the ocean, and I knew that if they dropped me, I would fall to my death.

Then, when I'd grown tired of screaming and pleading, and my throat was raw, they shot down to the ground of a dark forest, and left me.

I scurried to my feet, eyes wide as I surveyed my surroundings.

All I saw were tall trees, a dark sky above, and wet leaves below my feet. There was no snow. So, I assumed I was out of Tythra.

My eyes narrowed. I must be on the other side.

A hoarse cry came from my mouth as someone yanked me back by my hair. I was pulled to the ground. My lips trembled as a grotesque creature peered over me as they tied my arms and legs together.

Two more emerged from the shadows, crawling on their bony hands and feet like animals, but standing on two legs once they were close enough to look down at me. When they stood, they were little taller than a small man, and wearing tight clothes that barely covered their round bellies.

The three of them spoke to one another in a language I did not recognize. By the slippery, wet skin and bulbous eyes, I took them for goblins. Pity, Kala never taught me their language.

"Who?" One of them shouted to me. "Who? You."

I shook my head, confused.

He blew air through his thin lips. Then, he pointed to his chest. "Me, Grint." Then, he stabbed his finger into my ribs. "Who, you?"

Again, I shook my head. I wasn't going to reveal my identity.

The others pushed one another, obviously annoyed that they had no idea of who I was.

Grint sneered at me, then, lifted his head to the sky and whistled.

A weyr came darting through the sky and landed right above my head. It squawked and tucked its wings down by its side, then tapped its nose onto my forehead.

Disgusted, nausea bubbled in my stomach at the feel and smell of it.

They exchanged words. I didn't recognize any but one.

Aether.

Satisfied with the weyr's response, Grint gave a sharp, yellow-toothed grin down at me and waved the creature away.

I was lifted from the ground and tossed over the back of the one who tied me up. I prayed to the Guardians, begging for their help, as I was carried into the black forest.

CHAPTER 17

The Air Prince

"They took her," I yelled, and in the heat of rage, I lifted my metallic arm and called forth the power of the wind and storms.

The sky crackled with thunder and lightning and the electric threads wrapped themselves around the metal on my arm and raced up and down my body.

Teeth bared, I turned to the battle ensuing on the ship and cried out, releasing a force so powerful that the soldiers were sent flying back and the wind's howl grew deafeningly loud.

The weyrs tried to run, having gotten what they came for. But, no. I would not let them.

Outstretching my arm, the lightning shot out and struck each and every weyr around.

Queen Sorcha flew down to my side, gripping the edge of the ship.

"Go after her," she shouted to me, her green eyes full of desperation.

Kala bounded down the deck and growled. She shifted and stood, having transformed into her faerie form.

The glare she shot my way was enough to fill my body with ice.

"You let them take her," she accused, and I shook my head.

"I cannot go after her," I said. "If I tried, I would not be able to return."

"He's right," Queen Sorcha said. "None of us can cross over the way she can."

"The treaty means nothing anymore," Kala said. "We are at war with that monster. He cannot have my dear Celeste."

"Lowering her head, Queen Sorcha released a strangled cry.

"All is lost," I said, falling to my knees. I had her for such a short time and let her slip right through my fingers. Maybe I was never worthy. Perhaps it was all a joke, and none of us were what we thought.

The Guardians had chosen wrong.

"No," Kala said, her mouth twisting. "All is not lost."

Queen Sorcha and I shared a stunned glance and then looked to her.

"What do you mean?" I asked, coming to my feet. "Please tell me you know a way."

"We may not be able to cross over," Kala said, her eyes lifting to meet mine, as she released a heavy sigh. "But, I know someone who can."

CHAPTER 18

The Water Prince

The white gates of Allandria's capital city opened for us and Maxim and I stepped through on the back of two white horses. After days of travel, and with little sleep, I could not wait to be shown to my new private apartment.

Allandria was a breath of fresh air. The sun shone bright, and the lush, green landscape was a nice change from my kingdom of ice.

And soon, I would be united with the Aether.

We all would.

"We made it," I said, my smile beaming at the common-folk who welcomed us from the ground. Such happy faces.

"Indeed, we have, Stellan. In one piece," he said.

I chuckled. "I don't think I could have gone without you."

Maxim lifted his gaze to mine, his eyes troubled. "If I had died, you would have had to. For the sake of our world."

"I know. But, you're like a brother to me. This has always been our dream."

He looked ahead. "Some dreams aren't meant to come true."

What was wrong with him? He'd been gloomy and moody since the corsus attack. Though Maxim had never been particularly cheery or jovial, his demeanor was changed—his eyes cold.

Whatever happened to him that day left its mark. We'd saved his life, but I worried about his soul.

"What's the matter?"

He shrugged. "Nothing, I just want to get out of the saddle and into a hot bath."

"That's more like it," I said, as we slowed to a leisurely gait through the stone streets of the city. "Water is always cleansing and rejuvenating. Mother has always spoken about the natural springs and bath houses here."

He didn't reply, keeping quiet the rest of the trot up the winding roads that led to the palace.

After our arrival, we'd been shown to our rooms, and had been treated with the best service possible. Still, Maxim and I were a bit worried that my mother and the Aether hadn't returned.

My worst fears were realized when in walked, Queen Sorcha and Prince Ewan, without Princess Celeste Delacord.

CHAPTER 19

"**Y**ou've done some foolish things in the past, Stellan," My mother, Queen Sorcha said as she poured us a cup of tea. "But nothing like this. You could have gotten the both of you killed."

Maxim and I exchanged looks at each other, but kept silent.

She handed us two small, warm cup. "To think, you were infected by a corsus," she said, shaking her head. She stroked Maxim's cheek and smoothed his hair. "I can only imagine what you've been through."

"All is well," he said. "I'm fine now. I swear it."

I cleared my throat. "It had to be done, Mother. We couldn't leave without making sure Ever Frost was safe."

She spun on me, rage in her green eyes that matched mine.

"That's what the elders are for," she growled through clenched teeth. Then, she calmed herself, rubbing her temples. "You could have brought a corsus to Allandria. Don't you see what that means? That would have been a direct link between Emperor Jasper and our Aether. You could have destroyed all that the magic-born have worked for."

"We know," Maxim said. "We knew the risk."

"That's what worries me," she said, in a soft voice as she looked out the door of her balcony. "It's time for you to both to grow up." She rubbed her hands and she went silent for a moment.

Tension filled the room as we waited for our punishment. Maxim couldn't even look at me. Every time his eyes went in my direction, he quickly averted them. He was embarrassed and ashamed to have been the one left sick in bed for days.

The candles in the sitting room flickered as a soft breeze entered from one of the open balcony doors.

"The Aether is gone. While the dowager queen does everything she can to bring her back, we are all lost. As a mother, I should find a way to punish you. But, you two are Elementals, and my job as a mother was taken from me the day you became men. If the Aether finds her way back here by some divine intervention, I have to be confident that the two of you have learned your lesson, and will act accordingly. She needs you. We all do."

She glanced back and I caught a glimpse of tears in her eyes.

"Mother?"

Crossing the room, Queen Sorcha wiped her eyes. She paused before the door, composing herself. This was the first time I'd seen her look so upset. I missed her beautiful smile, the smile that gave me hope.

Maxim and I both watched as she opened the door, and Prince Ewan stepped inside the room. He was the most regal of us all, and a natural born warrior.

I had to admit, he was a bit intimidating, but we were supposed to be allies in all of this.

There was a war brewing, and we were the only soldiers who could fight in it.

"If you haven't noticed, one of us is missing," he said.

"Besides the Aether you lost?" Maxim asked, his voice stern.

He strode into the room, sword at his hip, metallic hand.

"It may be so," he said, nodding to us. "But, I'm here to talk about Prince Lancel, and what we will have to do if he doesn't show up."

CHAPTER 20

The Aether

Exhausted, I went in and out of sleep. I'd been carried for what felt like the entire day. Sun came and left, and I'd glanced up at it from over the shoulder of the goblin, in awe of the round ball of yellow light that I hadn't seen in years.

My captors cackled in the distance while I writhed against the ropes that bound my arms and legs together. Night fell, and while they sat by a fire, roasting rats, I was left alone with my hunger and fatigue.

Escape filled my mind, but, until I could free myself from their ropes, there wasn't much I could do.

"Come on, magic," I whispered, pleading. "Show yourself for once. Get me out of this mess."

My fingers tingled, and for a moment hope came to me. Then, I realized that it was just me losing the feeling in my hands from having my wrists tied tightly for the entire day.

Cold, hungry, I gave into the dark void that smothered me like a warm blanket.

Memories flooded back to me like a baby in its bassinet, and for the first time in years I had a dream that didn't incite fear or worry.

My fifth birthday was one of my favorites. It was just two years before my family and I were ripped from our home and forced into exile. It was before I even knew any danger was brewing.

At that age, life was a hectic collection of parties, new toys, lessons, and singing in front of my parent's guests. Singing had always been one of my true delights—one that even prison couldn't take away from me.

A grand party was being thrown for me at my grandmother's castle in the rural countryside of Mordigan. The white castle stood out against the clear, blue sky and bright sun.

Rolling green hills and meadows of pink flowers were outstretched on all sides for miles. A lake awaited at the bottom of the hill, full of fish and swans swimming amongst the lily pads.

I was dressed in a lovely blue gown with pearls and a cream sash tied at my waist. Rarely did I feel beautiful. In a land with pink-skinned faeries and girls with wings, I always felt like a brown, spotted duck amongst swans. But, on this day, I knew I was the prettiest faerie in all the land. I even managed to keep my hair blonde during the entire party.

Such happiness was a treasure, and I wished I'd have known what was coming. I would have cherished it.

My cousins were either too old or too young to play with me, but one boy was there who was just my age. Apparently, it was his birthday too. His mother had traveled with him from a kingdom far away to meet me and give me a gift.

Queen Sorcha, and Stellan, enjoyed the festivities along with everyone else in attendance. After the sun began to set and many of the guests began to leave, Queen Sorcha retreated back into the castle with my parents and grandparents to have a private discussion that I wasn't invited to join in.

I didn't mind. Stellan was there and all he wanted to do was play with me in the mazes.

"I'll show you the way," I had said with a grin, and after kicking off my slippers, I showed him to the back door of the maze.

The cobblestone walkway lead directly to the biggest maze on my grandparent's estate.

"Follow me," I said. "In the very center is the best garden you've ever seen."

"Not better than the one at my palace," Stellan said.

I ran along the path, holding my skirts. "I bet you it is!"

Stellan was faster. He flew ahead of me and I frowned, trying to run faster.

"No fair. Flying isn't allowed."

Stellan flew backward, his red hair rustling in the wind, and folded his arms across his gray suit jacket.

"I didn't know there were rules."

My breaths came out quicker, my legs started to burn, and the smell of fresh-cut flowers filled my nostrils. I was nearly there. I nodded and met him inside the maze. "Yes. There are always rules."

Stellan smirked. "Well, I have a rule for you."

I put my hands on my hips, and tried to catch my breath. "What rule?"

Stellan lowered to the ground and stood before me. At seven we were exactly the same height. I tried to stand a little straighter so that I would be taller than him. He lifted his feet off the ground until he was high enough to look down and give me a smug grin.

"Whoever gets to the garden in the center of the maze first, gets a prize."

I twisted my mouth in thought. "What prize?"

He giggled and took off into the maze without a reply.

I stomped my foot. "I told you that flying is not allowed," I shouted, and ran the opposite direction. Inside there was the smell of freshly trimmed bushes and trees. The tall hedges were like walls, causing anyone within to feel as though they were enclosed in a sweet smelling garden.

I forgot to mention that I didn't know my way to the center. I'd only been there with my grandmother.

I held tight to skirt, trying not to step on their trimmings as I searched through the maze of the garden, or at least Stellan so that I wouldn't feel so alone.

Green walls, composed of bushes, stood tall above my head, confusing me with their identical nature. My head, full of the blonde ringlets, quickly turned as I heard something behind me.

I smirked. "Are you lost?"

I stalked toward the sound, suppressing my laugh. A shock of cold water splashed into my face and I stood frozen with fear. I coughed and turned to run, gasping as I crashed directly into Stellan.

"Found a fountain in the center," he said, wrapped his arms around me, and lifted me into the air.

So much for keeping my hair blonde. It turned white as we went higher and higher. This was no longer fun. I was terrified as I wrapped my arms around his neck and pressed my face to his chest. I glanced down and saw that the ground was too far away.

"Don't drop me, Stellan!"

His laugh was loud and without restraint. Refreshing. "I am strong. I won't drop you. We are almost there."

I held on tightly as Stellan flew with me. The rush of air as we flew made my hair tickle my face.

"Look, Celeste!"

I opened my eyes and looked at Stellan's face. His smile almost calmed me. Still, I didn't feel secure in his arms. I swallowed and followed his gaze downward.

Below, I could see all of the maze. It was massive, with several hidden sections with gardens and small ponds, and a grand fountain in the center.

"Amazing," I said with wonder.

"Yes," Stellan said. He pointed to the gardens in the center. "They are pretty, but mine are still prettier."

"Take me there!"

"Promise me something first," Stellan whispered to me.

"What?"

"You and I will be king and queen together when we are older."

I laughed at him, thinking about how much I loved this game. I had no idea what he meant, but my mother and father were king and queen and they were the happiest people I knew. They loved each other and I wanted to be like them.

Stellan was as good as any boy.

"Yes. I promise. Now, take me down to the garden fountain. I'll show you how to swim like a mermaid."

Stellan smiled, held me tighter, and together we flew to the gardens.

It was one of the best days of my life.

"*How ridiculously boring*," an unfamiliar voice whispered, and the beautiful memory was sucked away in an instant as a hand clamped over my mouth.

CHAPTER 21

It was cold, and wet, like someone who had just gotten out of the bath or from a swim. The water dripped from whoever's face was before mine, and terror chilled me from within. My heart thumped in my chest as whoever was straddling my body sniffed my neck.

Why couldn't I see them?

The darkness was thick and all-consuming.

"Hmm," a male voice whispered. "You look like her. You smell like her. Are you *her?*"

I shook my head. *Who?*

"No," he said. "This will not do. I want to see you. Examine you."

Within seconds, a jolt tore me from the my spot on the forest floor and I found myself lying facedown in mud.

Shivering, and completely disoriented, I pushed myself to my knees. Everything was...different.

The goblins were nowhere to be found.

I sat on my hands and knees in the middle of a jungle. The tall trees were dark and still, and the sky was a dull red. I remembered skies that color. In the human realm, the sky would sometimes turn red in the summer.

Where was I?

The smell of rotting flesh and fresh rain mixed in a sickening scent that had me covering my nose.

A pile of charred logs appeared before me. From that, a stake appeared and my cheeks paled. Within the blink of an eye, two people screamed as flames licked and consumed them.

No.

The screams ended in an odd purr as the flames were sucked away, leaving the two people standing there, together, holding hands as they were tied to the stake.

Silence surrounded me as I mustered the courage to crawl closer and take a look. The crunching below my hands and knees only amplified the eerie quiet. Before I even got a look at the bodies, I already knew who they were. My heart thumped in my chest.

A cry strangled within my throat. "Father," I gasped, realizing that I was witnessing their deaths, in reverse. "Mother."

"No. No. No," the voice said, softly.

A cold sensation flooded my midsection when I reached out for her and was ripped back.

I crashed into the jungle floor with a thud and a grunt.

"That'll be enough. I just had to be sure."

My head pounded with pain and I tasted blood from biting my tongue.

"Blonde hair. Blue eyes. Her tiny nose. Yes. Yes. It *is* her."

His voice came closer, and I was awestruck by who I saw before me.

I had imagined a weyr, with wiry arms and legs too long for its body. Maybe rubbery wings with holes in it. Not the vision who stood before me, leaned back against a tree.

He was tall, with short hair the color of violets. The color was

so intense and radiant that he had to be fae. No—not just any fae
—Unseelie.

Wait. Realization filled my bones and seeped into my blood.

Jasper. The emperor of the dead. The ruler of The Veil.

Pensive amber eyes looked me up and down as the man
thought to himself.

I looked away. His chest was bare, and his tight abs almost
distracted me. With an olive skin tone, it made his hair and the
thick black line of paint across his eyes stand out more.

"Who told you it was okay to come back to the magic-realm? I
have a mind to snap the tiny threads of your brain and leave you
simple-minded." He chuckled, pushing himself off the tree and
crossing his arms over his chest. "No one would want to marry
you then."

The idea that he could destroy my intellect and sanity had me
clawing at my eyes to waken myself.

He snorted. "What are you doing? I was only joking. Pull yourself together, girl."

"Who are you? Where am I?"

He appeared before me, crouched like an animal. Feral. Wild.

"I asked first. Who are *you*?"

Swallowing, I shook my head. I didn't know what to say.

He grabbed me by the chin, and slowing came to his feet. He
lifted me from the ground, brows knitted together over the most
hypnotizing eyes I'd ever seen.

He snickered. "Why are so afraid? You're supposed to be this
magical creature with the power to smite me with just a look.
Have the Guardians gone soft and chosen a squishy little girl who
I can pull apart with my teeth? Did they not tell you who I am...
what I am?"

I shook my head, eyes wide as I peered down my nose at him.
He held me up with his arm outstretched as if I weighed nothing
more than a fallen twig with a curious flower he needed a closer
look at.

"You've come to destroy my world, haven't you?"

"Lies."

"I don't know what you're talking about."

"Tell me your name," he said. "Before I snap your neck."

"Princess Celeste Delacord," I sputtered, the fear of death loosening my tongue.

"Brilliant," he said, dropping me to the ground. "That's all I wanted to know. A pleasure to meet you, my queen."

He mocked a deep bow that flung his bangs into his eyes. They lifted to me and a wicked smirk came to his full lips.

"And, I am..." he tapped his fingertips to his lips. "Your humble servant."

My eyes darted around me, desperate for an escape. I didn't respond. Instead, I broke into a run.

His laughter filled the jungle as a rope flung around my body and he snatched me back. I fell into his hard chest and he turned me toward him. Our bodies shot across the clearing until my back was slammed into a tree. He pinned me, so close that our noses touched and his slick abs were pressed against my belly.

His canines lengthened and he licked them. "How about I change into what I really am and pick my teeth with your bones?"

I tensed, but fire filled my eyes as I looked back at him straight in the face. "You go ahead and try. I can destroy you with a blink of an eye. Don't make me do it."

For a moment, he was surprised, then amusement filled his expression. He let out a howl of a laugh. "You will do no such thing. Your power has yet to be awakened."

My blood ran cold. He knew. But, how?

"By the grace of the Guardians," he breathed into my neck. "You certainly smell delicious. Like fire, and innocence. How about you give me a taste? I'll awaken that burning flame within your soul. I'll show you what real power feels like."

I squeezed my eyes closed as his lips brushed mine. My breath was ripped away from my chest and I was awakened by someone shouting my name.

CHAPTER 22

"Celeste," Kala called, breaking me from the feverish sleep that gripped at me and held me down.

In a panic, my eyes opened, yet I was too weak to sit up. A heavy weight held me down.

Sunlight blinded me.

That was odd.

Kala's face blotted out the sun as she knelt and looked down upon me from her faerie form. There was nothing as comforting and beautiful as my grandmother's face, and she brought tears to my eyes.

"Am I dreaming?" I asked her, too afraid to hope.

My vision cleared as I tried to focus on her flawless face, tinged with a hint of cream mixed with magenta.

She stroked my cheek, tears in her eyes.

"You are safe now, Celeste. We have been blessed. Praise the Guardians for their generosity."

The Guardians? I had no memory of their part in all of this.

All I remembered was the scene of my parent's death and the dangerous man who taunted me.

"Where is he?" I asked, shooting up and clutching my throat. My eyes darted from side to side as I searched for him.

Tall. Handsome. Devilish.

To my relief, we were alone, in the middle of a meadow. The sun shone down on the honey wheat and warmed my face.

I touched my cheek. It had been ages since I'd felt its warm embrace.

"Who is he, dear? The Guardians have saved you and brought you back to me," Kala said, placing her hand on mine.

I covered her hand with my other, and held tight. I didn't want to ever let go again. I continued surveying this bright new world and wet my lips.

"Where are we?"

"Allandria, dear," she said, and my brows lifted. "You've made it. The Guardians have brought you back to me. I prayed, and prayed, and begged for them to intervene. None of us could go into The Veil to retrieve you, but they could. And, they did. Blessed be."

Tears burned my eyes, and though I wanted to forget their deaths with all of my heart, I also wanted to cling to the memory of their faces. I gasped and wept. I had forgotten what they looked like.

How could I?

My heart broke for the second time in my life.

"Oh, Kala. It was awful."

"What did you see?"

"I saw mother and father. Their deaths. Their suffering," I said, covering my face as I sobbed.

"You're here now. You have been saved and we have all been blessed. Now, let's hurry to the palace before they think to cancel the entire coronation."

It was all so vivid, and intense. Had the Guardians truly brought me back? Kala seemed to think so, and there I was in the blink of an eye.

Still, I could still smell him, feel him pressed against me. But, I didn't want to alarm her. I shrugged off the memory. I was safe now, and Jasper couldn't get his hands on me now that I was safe in the human realm.

Kala shifted into her wolf form, and motioned for me to get on her back.

Hesitant, I walked over to her. She was a great wolf, tall and regal. But, I never imagined riding on her back.

"Hurry, girl. We don't have much time to waste."

Those words sprung me into action, and I pulled myself onto her soft white fur, and held tight.

She took off, racing across the meadow, and I leaned forward, closing my eyes.

I drew in a long, slow breath of cleansing air and readied myself.

Here we go.

CHAPTER 23

As Kala and I entered the white gates of the city, my distracted thoughts melted into the back of my mind. A litter awaited us after Kala flew up to the palace and alerted Queen Sorcha of our arrival.

I sat inside the litter, nearly leaning over the side as I marveled at the sights. I'd been deprived of such beauty for far too long.

Opulent didn't begin to describe what Allandria truly was. The trees outstretched high into the heavens, and from their branches were hundreds of houses. Glass and gold combined with the wood of the trees and glittered as traces of sunlight peeked through the forest canopy.

The roads were paved in cream stone, and the river flowed around the city, like a moat, but full of life and beauty.

"Good gracious," I said, as iridescent fish jumped and played in the river, their scales shimmering in the light.

Set in the center of the bustling city, the Allandrian Palace stood at the center of the empire. The cream and gold of the palace's siding shone beneath the bright, blue sky.

It was the most delightful thing I'd seen in ages. Memories of

Mordigan returned to me as I recalled swimming in the koi pond and splashing my mother as she sat on the edge, reading. Always reading. My smile faded. I'd seen her perish, and it had not been merciful.

Once we reached the palace, Prince Ewan and Queen Sorcha were there with two other young men, eagerly awaiting our arrival.

By the look on his face, I could see relief in Prince Ewan's eyes and a visible release of tension in his face as he approached. He took my gloved hand and helped me to the stone walkway.

"My dear," he said. "I have been sick with worry. If I could have jumped over the side of the ship and gone after you, I would have."

I nodded, forcing a smile. "I know. There was nothing you could have done against him," I said, and he tensed.

"Against who?"

I pursed my lips, my eyes locking with those of who I knew to be Stellan's.

"Nothing," I said, and left him to approach the boy from my dream, my childhood friend.

He was a remarkable specimen. Dark red hair and blue eyes, but there was a thick red beard that hadn't been there before. I smiled as I approached him and gave it a tug.

He lifted his brows, gazing down at me with a surprised look on his face.

"Hello, fathead," I said, searching his eyes.

The smile that greeted me warmed my heart. It was all worth it.

"And, hello to you stinky-face," he said, and we chuckled together, embracing tightly. He spun me around and I held on as if I held on for life, joy filling my entire body.

It was just as we'd left it as children.

I was home.

My eyes left his to meet those of the young man beside him.

"And, who are you?" I asked, reaching my hand out to him.

He took my hand and kissed the knuckles. "I am Prince Maxim of Kyushu. Pleased to meet you."

"The Earth Prince," I said. I'd felt his energy, perhaps stronger than the others. I just didn't know why. "Pleased to meet you as well."

"This way, princess. We need to prepare you for the coronation," Queen Sorcha said, and ushered us into the palace. "Come, meet your ladies-in-waiting and get acquainted with the traditions of the coronation."

"See you at dinner, my queen," Maxim said, leaving a lingering kiss on my knuckles once more.

Something stirred within me, and I was locked in his gaze. "I'll look forward to it," I said in a soft voice as I was led away by Queen Sorcha.

Two guards waited outside, with their swords sheathed and their armor polished. As I stared at them, they barely blinked or moved an inch.

"Beautiful, isn't it?" Prince Ewan asked, approaching from behind.

"Yes," I said. "Quite."

He looked down at me, a twinkle in his eyes.

I nodded, though its beauty only brought back painful memories of a life I had been stolen from.

"Ostrum Palace isn't nearly as grand as this," he added. "Drab and older than dirt."

"Will I see it someday?"

He lifted a brow. "If you'd like. I must apologize for my brothers and their manners in advance."

Nodding, together we walked up the gray, stone staircase to the open archway that led inside the palace.

"Welcome to your new home," Queen Sorcha said. She smiled

at me and smoothed my hair. "Until your coronation, you'll be guarded at all times and will remain in the palace. Its for your protection. We can't have anyone ruining our plans. Not after everything we've done to get you two here."

"When will my coronation be exactly?" I asked.

For a moment, I didn't think I sounded like myself. Jasper had done what he'd threatened; he'd awakened something within me. A fire and a forwardness I didn't know existed. I would survive, and as queen, I would have the power to destroy him.

She glanced over her shoulder, just at the base of the stairs, her eyes narrowing. "Eager, aren't we?"

I looked at her, unblinking.

"Tomorrow," she said, leading the way up the winding staircase, and my face flushed.

"So soon?" I asked and Prince Ewan gave my hand a squeeze.

"Yes," she said. "Once the sun sets on the end of the Solstice, our chance to bind you won't come again for another ten years."

"My goodness," I said, releasing a heavy sigh. "I had no idea."

"Well," she said. "You've been gone for weeks. We are short on time."

I clasped my hand over my mouth. "Weeks?"

She looked to me, brows furrowed. "A journey through The Veil does not happen at the same pace as our time, my dear. We have all been worried sick. And yes, for weeks."

My stomach sank. Why didn't Kala tell me? She'd been waiting there, praying, pleading with the Guardians to save me.

I realized what a task it had been, and as I glanced back down at her as she waited outside, I couldn't help but love her even more.

My legs burned from hiking up nine flights of stairs, but I was surprised that I wasn't more afraid. One day I would be an empress, and all of my years of sorrow and suffering would be behind me.

Allandria was mine, and I wanted to know her and study every part of her. So, I observed every floor as we went steadily upward.

I was surrounded by dimly lit corridors with ceilings that reached to the sky. Statues seemed to watch me, as did paintings of people with the same grim look on their face.

My heart raced a bit, thumping in my chest like a drum. I hadn't had so much free space to wander since childhood.

Once we reached my private apartment, Queen Sorcha opened the double doors and we walked into a room full of light.

"Princess, please meet Morgan, Talia, Simi, and Lena," she said, and four beautiful faeries all curtsied before me.

"Hello," I said, and the queen and Ewan turned to leave the room.

Ewan stopped to kiss my cheek, and stroked the back of my hand. "See you at dinner."

I nodded, forcing a smile despite the heavy worry that weighed me down. "See you then, my prince."

"Take good care of her," Queen Sorcha said to my ladies-in-waiting.

"We will," they said in unison, and once the doors closed.

"I'm Morgan," said the faerie with the black hair and purple skin.

Her eyes were a bit too big for her face, but the most beautiful shade of gray I had ever seen. She lifted my shirt over my head while another unbuckled my belt.

"Pleasure to finally meet you, your royal highness," she said.

"Likewise," I said as someone began tugging at my hair. "Ouch!"

"Oops," said the one with the pink hair and dark, brown skin. She smiled at me, pink eyes cast down in apology. "My apologies, your royal highness. I am Talia."

I learned that the two brunettes were identical twin sisters, Simi and Lena, as they took began tugging my clothes and shoes off until I was naked and covering my private areas in the middle of the room.

"Oh, don't be shy, your royal highness," Morgan said, her eyes meeting mine. "We'll make you shine for your handsome princes. Just leave it to us."

CHAPTER 24

The day had raced by in a whirlwind. As night fell, I couldn't help but worry if I was ready to truly lead an empire.

"Look at them," I said to Kala, who stood beside me in her gown, casting a regal gaze upon the ball held in the Elemental's honor. "They scare me."

Her white hair was twisted into a bun that matched her evening gown. In a sea of white where everyone but the Elementals wore the same lavender and ivy, me and the princes stood out. It made it easy for the guests to find us and wish us well.

"Do not worry, I will always be here to protect you," she said.

I played with the purple stone on the necklace around my neck. My cheeks flushed every time someone from my court nodded in my direction or approached for conversation. With sweaty palms, I tried my best to emulate my grandmother's poise, though my heart thundered in my chest.

This was what it would be like for the rest of my life. I'd better get used to it.

"Down there," she said. "Are the Faust sisters. Their family openly challenged your rule. Watch out for them."

Curious, I stared at them, wondering what they thought of me and if they'd present a problem.

As if sulking, they remained in the back of the packed hall of the palace on a bench against the velvet draped walls.

Triplets, with pale skin, black hair, and dark eyes. They were the picture of sinister beauty.

Prince Ewan walked up the stairs to the balcony and stood at my other side, hands resting on the railing.

"So," he said. "How does it feel to know you will be queen of all that you see, and much more?"

I touched my throat, and laughed, nervously.

"Its all a bit intimidating, honestly."

Kala leaned over to kiss my cheek. "I shall retire for the night, my dear. Do not stay out too late, you must be rested for the days to come."

I nodded to her. "Good night."

Ewan and I watched her walk away, and shift back into a wolf once she was out of the reception hall.

While I waited on the balcony, Stellan worked the room. He was made for being the center of attention, and I watched him, taking notes.

Once he stood on the opposite side of the room, in a balcony that faced mine, our eyes met and I gave him a nod and a smile. Stellan was the picture of perfection. His chiseled features made him look more like a work of art sculpted by the Guardians.

But, the tall figure standing in the shadows behind him intrigued me more than anyone in the entire palace.

Maxim.

My attention was diverted by the handsome half-human as Stellan raised a fist and tilted his head. He nodded at his hand with one lifted brow, making sure that I was paying attention.

"What is that trickster, Stellan up to?" Ewan asked.

I smiled, intrigued. Stellan opened his hand, a white dove

escaped his palm, and flew over the heads of all of our future subjects.

My eyes widened with delight as the bird flew to me. I wanted to catch it, but before my eyes, it swirled into a folded piece of paper.

"How did he do that?"

Ewan glanced down at the paper floating before my eyes. "Simple magic. Nothing more. Open it, quickly though," he said. "Before the spell fades."

I did as I was told, picking the paper from the air in front of me, and opening its simple folds. I read the words he'd written and relief washed over me.

Meet me in the garden.

My eyes flashed with mischief. I looked up at him with a grin on my face, and nodded.

CHAPTER 25

S tellan sat with me under the stars in the garden. We watched the statue in the fountain pour crystalline water into the pool.

"Tell me," he said. "What do you think of all this?"

I sighed, and looked down at my hands. "Well," I began. "Just look at me. My hair is styled in a fashion I've never seen, and I'm wearing the most expensive gown I could have dreamed of. But, under it all, I feel like a fraud."

He narrowed his eyes and took my hands into his.

"No, don't say such things. I can feel that this is right," he said, tracing the lines of my palms with his fingertips. "Can't you?"

My lips parted as I focused. I did feel it, something ancient and feral.

Magic.

He lifted his hand, and with it came a wave of water that took the shape of a mermaid. I gasped, then smiled with joy.

The mermaid looked at me with glossy eyes, and smiled, then waved at me before submerging into the water.

Stunned, I looked from the water, to Stellan. "How did you do that?"

He grinned with a shrug. "Water is my element, my love. But, with you here, holding my hand, just being in my presence, I can feel my power is getting stronger."

My shoulders slumped. "You do, but where is my power? I don't feel anything yet."

He took my face in his hands and kissed my forehead. "Give it time. You are the Aether. Maybe it isn't as simple as you think. Maybe it comes after you wear the crown."

My brows lifted. I never thought of it that way.

"You really think so?"

"I do. Just think of it this way. The Aether is said to hold so much power that it could reshape the world or even create new ones. It would make sense to ration it to you or wait until you were truly ready to wield it."

"Remarkable," I said. "You may be on target, fathead."

I couldn't help myself. It was a joy to be playful again. I'd missed out on so much of my childhood, that Stellan was the physical embodiment of the essence of that era.

He chuckled. "You're the only one I've ever let call me names like that."

"Good," I said, lowering my voice as he held my hand.

We both turned when out of the side doors of the palace walked Maxim. He waited in the shadows, as if waiting his turn to have time alone with me.

I had to admit, I was intrigued by him. During dinner, he'd been quite, almost pensive, and watched me with such curiosity that at times my cheeks burned with nervousness.

It was time to learn more about the shy prince.

"Until tomorrow," Stellan said, and we stood.

He lead me to Maxim, and bowed to us both.

"Night," he said.

Maxim raked a hand through his long hair. "Night, Stellan."

Then, he turned to me. For a moment, there was an awkward silence, and I forced a smile.

"Come, fair prince," I said, taking the lead and hooking my arm around his. Two shy people would get nowhere. "Let's take a stroll around the gardens."

CHAPTER 26

The Earth Prince

I t was unreal. After all of those years waiting to meet her, we
were in the same place together.

"Tell me about yourself," Celeste said as we walked side
by side through the garden courtyard.

A week had passed since the corsus attack, and Makya had
assured me that Star no longer infected my body, but, it didn't
ease my worries.

Celeste was everything to me, and I could not risk her life.

The nightmares of Star and what it would do to Celeste
haunted me. For a moment, I contemplated telling her all that
happened, but fear of somehow alerting Star of my whereabouts
just by speaking its name kept me silent.

I shifted my thoughts to the beautiful young woman beside
me. In a red gown, she was a vision, one I never wanted to forget,
so I studied her—the curves of her hips, the mounds of her full
bosom, the perfection of her face.

"I was born in Kyushu," I said, rubbing my jaw. "Its a small
kingdom, but beautiful. It's mostly mountains, with some active

volcanoes, but none close to the villages. There are these cherry blossoms that bloom every spring and the people would celebrate with grand balls and festivals.

Ancient temples of worship stood amongst the forests in all corners of the kingdom. White rushing rivers my father and I would raft through whenever we pleased. And, rice fields that stretched for miles. You've never seen anything like it, my dear Celeste."

She smiled at me, and my heart melted. How could one fall for someone so hard that they'd just met hours ago? I did not have an answer, but I deducted that it was fate—a theory that had no proof or an quantifiable evidence.

"Sounds lovely," she said.

I returned the smile. "It was." Then, my smile faded. "Until it was discovered that my mother was a faerie, and I was born of human and magic-born blood. The people revolted. After centuries upon centuries of kindness and peace, that simple detail made them turn against the royal family."

She took my hand into hers, but kept silent. Such grace and manners. I gave her hand a squeeze and went on.

"My parents were killed, and I only escaped because a palace servant took pity upon me and smuggled me out of the kingdom in a crate marked to have rice."

Celeste stopped, and turned to me.

My breaths came out ragged as she wiped tears from my cheeks. I didn't even know I had began to cry, and roughly ran my sleeve across my face, embarrassed.

She took my face between her hands and gazed into my eyes.

"Its all right, Maxim," she said. "My parents were killed right in front of me as well. I know the pain you feel. If you think about it, we are more alike than any of the other Elementals. We are bound by our suffering and those awful memories."

She took my breath away with her words—her understanding.

I couldn't help myself. I kissed her then, so passionately and forcefully that I barely recognized myself or my actions. Her lips were soft as rose petals, and mine burned against hers until I wasn't sure if I was breathing my air or hers.

Was it the power that connected us, or something else?

I didn't care. I grabbed her by the hips and carried her to the stone wall that reached high into the clouds. We were alone, and the sweet sounds of night filled the warm air as I devoured her mouth.

She didn't resist. Though a day had passed between our meeting, it had been years of torture and agony waiting for that moment. Our power bound us, made us sense each other and crave union. It screamed for us to touch, the way my body begged for hers.

Her hands laced into my hair, tugging in a delicious mixture of need and excitement as I took her bottom lip between my teeth and traced it with my tongue.

There was no resisting the yearning that burned in my heart for her, or the filling of blood in my manhood. She'd awakened a side of me I never knew existed. Years of study, training, devotion to my craft were nothing compared to the desire to make her mine.

Like an animal, I licked at her white throat and slid my hands up her skirts. Her soft flesh was warm beneath my palms, her bottom round, yet firm.

When she wrapped her legs around my waist, I tore her from the wall and guided her to the soft grass.

"The guards," she breathed into my ear. "They'll see us."

My fingers found their way to such delicious wetness that I couldn't wait to taste it the way I'd tasted her mouth.

"I care not," I said, and her giggle rang in the night air as I slid my fingers into her hot core and stroked her until those enchanting blue eyes of hers rolled back and she cried out my name.

CHAPTER 27

The Aether

I awoke to the sun's light spilling into my room as Morgan pulled the drapes open and stood beside my bed with a smile on her lips.

"Morning, your highness," she said with a curtsy.

Blushing, I covered my face with the blanket. Prince Maxim's arms were still wrapped around me, as mine were holding onto a down-filled pillow that was still cool against my face while his body was hot pressed into my back.

"Breakfast will be served in your chamber if you'd like. And then, we must prepare for the coronation."

"Yes," I said. "That would be lovely. Thank you."

She curtsied again and left the room, closing the double doors.

I rolled over and examined his sleeping face. How he slept through all of that was beyond me, but I was grateful for it. I wanted a chance to study him, unabashed. Without limit.

He was terribly handsome. Dark skin and long lashes that stuck straight out. I smiled. I even liked his the freckles on his cheekbones.

This is what humans looked like. Not much different from the fae, but equally as beautiful as the best of us. Tall, and lean, he was so different from the other princes. For a moment, I dared to think I liked him best.

I shook that idea away, ashamed. I was to love them equally. But, after the night of intimacy we'd shared, our bond was stronger for it.

I bit my bottom lip, he'd shown me such pleasure with just his mouth and fingers, I couldn't help but imagine the joys the rest of his body could show me.

He opened his eyes, the bright green almost illuminating the dimness beneath the covers.

"Were you watching me sleep?"

Snickering, I shook my head.

"Liar," he said, and kissed my forehead. He sat up to stretch. When he looked back at me, a curious grin came to his lips. "Well, that is quite interesting. Does your hair truly blush?"

He pointed at my hair and I paled when I pulled a handful outward to see it had gone from blonde to pink.

"Grace of the Guardians," I said, mortified. "It hasn't done that in ages."

He laughed and put a hand on my shoulder and turned me to look at him. My mouth opened with wonder when his eyes went from green to gold, to purple, and then completely black. He winked at me and returned them to their original color.

"We all have our little quirks," he said. "Yours isn't as unique as you'd probably thought."

I stared at him, still awestruck as he stepped from my bed and stretched his long arms over his head. His arms were corded with muscle and his back was tight and toned. Swallowing, I looked away.

"You'd better leave," I said. "Before Kala finds out you were here."

He glanced over his shoulder, pulling his shirt back on and buttoning the tiny buttons. "We are bound by power," he reminded me. "We can do whatever we want."

"But, not married yet," I replied in turn. "We weren't supposed to be…intimate until after the coronation."

Bowing, his face went to one of seriousness. "As you wish, your royal highness. I will see you at sunset."

I licked my lips, taming a beaming smile. He began to leave, but rushed back to my bed, hopped in and placed a kiss on my lips.

"Just one more," he said. "And, I'll let you be."

I giggled, and watched him leave.

Once he was gone, Morgan and Talia entered the room. It was all business, and I was left to my thoughts as they fussed over me.

They tugged at my nightgown and then ushered me into the outer chamber where a hot bath was drawn, sectioned away from the rest of my apartment by antique room dividers with elaborate embroidery of roses and vines.

My ladies-in-waiting bathed me in perfumes and oils, brushed and braided my hair into the current Allandrian style for the ladies of high breeding and royalty.

This was all so new to me, the servants, the tradition, the attention from handsome men.

Being with a man was something I had been told was a possibility, but I still never truly believed I would ever be set free from the Crimson Tower.

Not alive, at least.

Morgan went over to the large wardrobe beside the bedroom door and pulled out an elegant black gown.

My jaw dropped as I looked at the rich fabric and touched it with my fingertips.

"Its amazing," I said, in awe.

"It's your coronation dress," she said. "Let's fit you."

As she pulled the dress over my head, it all began to become real. I gawked at my reflection in the mirror. Yesterday, I was pretty. Today, I was beautiful.

Within hours, I would rule all of the magic-realm.

CHAPTER 28

Afternoon came, and it was time—time to claim my throne before the entire court.

Queen Sorcha waited for me at the doors that led into the throne room.

She took me by the hands and kissed both of my cheeks.

"Are you ready?"

I sucked in a breath of air. "I do hope so."

She gave me a stern look. "You better be. We've waited long enough for this."

"But, what if I am not the one?"

She sighed, and shook her head. Then, her face softened as she looked at me.

"I know you are afraid. There is a lot of responsibility on your shoulders. But, do not fret. You are back, and the Guardians have assured us that the prophecies will be fulfilled. You are the Aether, the supreme Elemental," she said, tucking a fallen strand of hair behind my ear. "Now, it's time to meet your future court."

Inside, the people of court were waiting for us.

I took in a cleansing breath, and a foreign confidence settled upon me.

Head held high, I walked down the purple carpet of the throne room to the row of thrones set side by side. My ladies-in-waiting were at my side, keeping my long black gown from touching the floor. It was as though I walked on air, and from the looks on the courtiers faces, they were enchanted.

The air was cool from the open glass ceiling, and fragrant with the scent of burning All Season candles that were traditionally used for formal events such as this.

There was no yelling or expletives being shouted my way because I was what was considered a dark faerie. Instead, they bowed, some even cried, and the smiles that surrounded me made my heart swell with joy.

In the center was the most elaborate, with the wings of a dragon and a black back that looked like a portal or door to an enchanted place. I marveled at the embellishments and intricate designs.

Two female faeries played harps on either side of the platform of thrones, and elders soon assembled in cloaks of gold and black, jeweled crowns on their heads.

Faeric children sang in the back of the room, their voices so pure and magical, that one couldn't help but embrace the joy of this day.

The banners of Allandria stood on either side of the platform, and above hung a glorious chandelier that dripped with crystals and jewels that multiplied the bright light shining through from the glass ceiling.

As I sat on the throne, my heart thumped in my chest. I was the center of the magic realm. The ruler of them all.

In walked the princes, and a smile came to my face.

Prince Ewan never looked better. In his black suit with silver buttons and his sword at his side, he was regal as ever. He was followed by Stellan and Maxim, who both wore white.

Stellan carried his golden scepter, and to my surprise, he'd shaved his red beard revealing smooth skin and a charming white-toothed smile.

Maxim had pulled his long brown hair back into a ponytail at his nape, and kept his head down as he passed by the great crowd.

He was shy. I liked that about him—it was almost as if he didn't know he was one of the most attractive men I'd ever seen. When he lifted his eyes to meet mine and gave me a wink, my heart skipped a beat. Our evening in the garden would be forever cherished, and the memories made butterflies flutter in my belly.

They took their seats beside me and one was left empty at the very end. We exchanged looks, as did the crowd. The fire prince was not coming.

Shoulders slumping, I tried my best to not let my disappointment show. Everything had gone as planned, and it seemed that one elemental did not heed the call of the Guardians.

A gasp spread across the room as in flew a black dragon from the open ceiling. Magnificent, with large ebony wings, silver talons, amber eyes, and scales that glistened with a purple hue, he commanded attention from every being in attendance.

My hands gripped the chair and my back pressed to the throne.

My eyes widened as he landed right before me, and with a spin of flames and magic, he swirled and shifted into that of a handsome faerie—one I'd seen before.

Jaw slack, and breath caught in my throat, I beheld the enigmatic dark faerie as he bowed before me, a smug grin on his face. Those amber eyes that had struck terror and desire within me locked with mine as he took my hand and pressed his lips to my knuckles.

"Your majesty," he said as he stood.

"May I introduce, the Fire Prince," Queen Sorcha said, and my brows furrowed.

"Prince Lancel from House Visyrean," he said. "Son of Queen Isadora. Heir to the throne of Inaeza. Your savior."

"You cheeky bastard," I said. "Why didn't you tell me? You let me think you were Jasper."

He chuckled. "Is that what you thought? No, it is just I, your humble fire prince. You can thank me for returning you to your grandmother later."

My eyes widened. *What?* He had brought me back?

Cocky as ever, he strode down the platform and took his seat, hanging his legs over the arm and casting a self-satisfied gaze at the faeries of Allandria.

I covered my mouth. There were two Unseelie faeries in the Allandrian Court. This was unprecedented. Then, I nodded to Queen Sorcha who held the Dragon Crown in her hands.

I understood what a momentous event this was. What it meant to our people.

For the first time in centuries, the Seelie and the Unseelie Court were united. Light meets dark.

The Shadow Court.

Thanks for reading! I hope you enjoyed Court of Shadows. If you did, please consider leaving a review here.
Book Two, Court of Dragons will be released late spring.
Please, check out my other epic fantasies, Half-Blood Dragon and Fallen Empire! Both feature strong female leads, dragons, magic, and adventure.
Stay up-to-date by joining my mailing list here.

The Fire Prince

I watched her—pensive and intrigued. Every beat of her heart was as loud as a drum in my ears.

Who was this mysterious faerie who convinced me to abandon my sense of logic?

I was a warrior, a skilled Dreamweaver, and dragon. How is it that she'd seduced me into leaving my home and uniting with my mortal enemies?

Despite her serene face, her anxiety and apprehension wafted from her soul, burning my nostril hair. I wanted to snatch her away, fly her to the top of the Allandrian Mountains, and show her what *real* fear looked like. I could take her to the place where nightmares were weaved, and make her confront her darkest fears.

I had done it once, I could do it again—to show her what was truly at stake.

Ruling a nation of magic-born fae was nothing compared to the evil I'd seen. Still, there was something powerfully intoxicating about her.

The fact that she'd spent half of her life imprisoned did little to quench the need I'd suppressed all of those years. Though I'd been thousands of miles away in another realm, I felt her presence most nights, and resisted as long as possible.

Who wanted to become a slave to destiny—to a preordained life of servitude to one woman? It wasn't in me to be anyone's puppet. I was the heir to the Inaezan Throne, a kingdom of dragons.

We bowed to no one.

Yet, here I was, sitting in an embellished throne of gold and silver, waiting to be summoned to make my vow to her.

Memories of watching her claw her way to the ghostly image of her dying parents haunted me. Her tear-streaked face and wail of sorrow. It was then that the coldness of my heart began to melt for her.

Scratching my chin, I realized why I'd gone against my instincts, and chose to become part of her court.

As the crown was lowered onto her pretty little head, I knew I had to protect her. I knew I couldn't stand by while the evil of the world broke her spirit and stole her innocence. Someone had to look after her.

That someone was me.

The other Elementals were quiet, stoic young men without a clue of what went on in the Unseelie Court, or what happened in the Land of the Dead. They knew nothing of the darkness of one's heart—but, I did.

With a sigh, I sat up tall, clasping my hands across my lap as I leaned forward and continued watching her.

She was my destiny, and I had to keep her safe—keep her from *him*.

A LOOK AT COURT OF DRAGONS

The Aether

With the crown on my head, I knew that life would be forever changed. They watched me—the Shadow Court, but my heart thumped in my chest at the realization that I was the supreme ruler.

The first in centuries.

With the four princes standing on either side, I stood before the court and bowed my head as Queen Sorcha and Kala raised their wands and tapped them to the crown on my head and each of my shoulders.

"By Elahe, the Mother who gave her life so that the fae may live, and our sacred gods of Aden, we name you the Aether," Queen Sorcha said. "Empress Celeste Delacord, supreme ruler of Rune and the Magic-Born."

Those words sent chills up my arms and neck, and I tensed as my eyes lifted to hers, lashes fluttering as I swallowed a lump in my throat.

She smiled at me, but I saw doubt in her eyes. How I prayed I wouldn't disappoint her and everyone else who depended on me.

After the coronation, a procession was led through the streets of Allandria. We would weave our way down the stone pathway through the city, where I would come face-to-face with my subjects.

This was unlike anything I'd ever dreamed of. There was no hiding, no escape from the eyes that fell upon me.

In my black dress, I walked at a steady pace behind Queen Sorcha as the sun began to set above us. I smiled and waved, acknowledging the hordes of faeries who had come to the center of the city to gaze upon their new Empress.

They wore their most colorful, and fine garments, and raised their wands with joy as we made our way through, to the steady beating of drums.

"How does it feel?" Lancel asked, walking close to my left side. "You are the first to rule over the entire realm—the first in centuries."

His shoulder brushed mine—and just like in my dream, electricity jolted up my body—almost leaving me breathless.

"It doesn't feel real," I whispered, and wet my lips. My mouth and throat had gone dry, yet the palms of my hands were slick with sweat.

"Do you know what happened to the last Aether?"

I lifted a brow, mouth gone dry. "There was another?"

He scoffed. "Of course. Did you think you were special?"

Frowning, I looked away.

Perhaps I did.

"Yes. She was said to be beautiful and powerful—what powers do you have, exactly?"

My face heated. He was goading me. He knew I hadn't exhibited any true magic quite yet.

Chuckling, he went on. "Do not worry. I know its in there... somewhere. I could feel it—smell it when I walked in your dream. I dare say I have never felt anything like it. Maybe one day I'll get a taste of it."

My cheeks burned, yet I pursed my lips and tried to ignore him.

"What? You did know that you'll have to choose one of us to be your mate, didn't you?" he said, giving me a sidelong gaze.

He smirked when I swallowed a lump in my throat. Of course, I'd given it some thought. There were four princes in my court, and I'd been promised as a potential wife to them all. None could move on and marry until I made a choice.

How was I expected to do such a thing?

The only one I knew prior to this all was Stellan, and he felt more like a brother than anything. Then, there was Maxim and I couldn't help but admit that my entire body craved his touch every time he looked at me.

Ewan was handsome, and gallant, but we hadn't had much time together since sailing across The Veil. I did yearn to learn more about him, and couldn't wait for a chance to do so.

Lancel, on the other hand, irritated and made me uncomfortable whenever he was around. He was the last prince I'd choose, that much I was certain of.

"We may all be in your court, and will share the responsibility of protecting the realm, but our betrothal began with our births, and you cannot bare all of our children, silly girl. One. That's all you get, ultimately."

"I wish you'd stop talking," I said, through clenched teeth.

"Not a fan of sound advice, are you?"

"I want to do my duty and protect the realm."

"Certainly," he said. "You'll do well. Or, they'll crucify you if you prove unworthy."

I shot him a glare. "How could you say such a thing?"

Shrugging, he looked ahead. "I speak the truth. Would you rather I lied? Oh, dear Empress, they love you—eternally and without question. Rubbish."

Snapping my mouth closed, I walked faster, eager to get as far away from him as possible without sparking any controversy. As I pulled ahead of the princes, I couldn't help but admit that he was right.

I knew it.

Everyone knew it.

I still had to prove myself.

After the procession through the city, we returned to the palace. I was still in a bit of a solemn mood when Stellan pulled me into a quiet corridor.

Stunned, I looked at him with widened eyes. I was tired and ready for bed.

But, when I noticed the mischievous grin on his face, I couldn't help but bring a curious smile to mine.

"What are you up to?" I asked, folding my arms across my chest. Despite my suspicion, I was incredibly intrigued, and suddenly had more energy than merely seconds before.

He looked from right to left, and around the corner of the wall to make sure no one was around in earshot. Then, he turned his bright green-eyed gaze back on me and bit his bottom lip in the sexiest way possible.

"I'm kidnapping you," he said, wriggling his brows.

"What?"

He laughed and pulled me along. "You'll see."

A LOOK AT FALLEN EMPIRE

They say the Age of Dragons ended after the War on Magic, but hiding in the forgotten lands remains one clan destined to reclaim their ancestral home.

While Kylan hunts firedrakes by day, he prepares for a journey across the Sea of Dreams where mermaids thrive and the key to his people's survival is prophecized to be hidden.

Amalia, a Mage, escaped The Brotherhood, a sect of monks who seek the descendants of the gods. Now, unable to return to neutral territory where magic-users are safe, she finds herself fighting for survival amongst men who can turn into wolves, firedrakes, and a relentless monk who believes she can restore balance to the entire world.

For Amalia, the gods are not just a memory. They are her ancestors, and before she can learn to control her newfound gift, she will face the keeper of a forgotten empire.

A dragon.

In this sprawling epic fantasy novel with shifting wolf hybrids, dragons, and mermaids, Amalia's first battle is for more than her life. It's for the souls of every being born with magic. Join New York Times bestselling author, K.N. Lee on an adventure perfect for fans of Vikings and Game of Thrones.

From Chapter One

A FIRST KISS was supposed to be special. Memorable. As Tomas pulled away from Amalia, her eyes opened with confusion.

Is that it?

Her silver-gray eyes filled with disappointment.

Was that what she'd been waiting for all of her life?

The taste of onion was on his tongue, and the coarse feel of chapped lips didn't help the experience.

He gave her a grin—a gap-toothed one she had hoped she'd grow to appreciate, maybe even love one day.

Amalia couldn't afford to be picky. Though Tomas wasn't the most handsome, or even the smartest lad in the village, he had proclaimed his love for her. He knew a trade and was kind.

She licked her lips and forced a tight smile.

He'd have to do.

It was a fact that not many would even consider marrying a Mage. Especially one like Amalia—one marked by the gods. Not when Mages were being hunted down by Wolves, or even worse, the Brotherhood.

Skal was neutral territory. But, invisible borders meant nothing when the people within them held the same prejudice as those outside.

"So," he said, his cheeks reddening. "What do you think?

"It was lovely," she lied, blinking.

The look of relief on his face was reassuring. Within a month's time, Amalia would be fifteen and of age. She'd be Tomas' wife.

"Good," he said. "I can't tell you how long I've waited for this moment. Seems like all of my life. For as long as I could remember. At night, all I can think of are the way your eyes remind me of the night sky, and how I'd give anything to look into your eyes every day until the day I die."

Her smile turned genuine. She should set aside her selfish vanity and desire for a handsome boy, one who would make her heart sing. The time for silly childish ideas about what life would hold was coming to an end. It was time for her to accept her fate and prepare for a simple life with a simple man.

"I had no idea," she said, reaching out for his hand.

"Of course, you didn't. You barely looked at me until our parents made the arrangement."

She ran her fingers through the tangles of her hair. Somehow the long, black strands always seemed to knot around one another. "That's not true. You are a very nice young man. Any girl would be happy to have you."

"That's nice of you to say. But, I know I'm not a knight or a raider or anything special like that."

"It is the truth. I can't think of anyone kinder than you in the village," she said and glanced at the paling sky. The smell of rain was faint in the air, but the clouds were darkening by the minute. "Perhaps we should return to the village. It looks like a storm is coming this way."

He followed her gaze, combing his long dark hair from his mahogany-colored eyes. "I think you're right." He reached for her hand. She accepted and he pulled her to her feet.

She brushed grass from her faded blue gown and gray smock and stretched her arms above her head. By the bubbling brook at the foot of the Weeping Mountain, they had feasted on ripe mango and warm honey bread her mother had prepared for their first excursion alone as intended mates.

Tonight, there would be a feast. Their families would dine together and their fathers would discuss matters of joining their resources.

It was the way of the Skal.

A way Amalia wished she could forever be free of.

Together, they gathered their blanket and basket, and the scent of burning wood wafted their way.

Her brows furrowed as she stood to her full height—almost as tall as Tomas.

"What's wrong?"

She sniffed the air. "Do you smell something?"

"I do, actually," he said, frowning. "What is that? Is something burning?"

The air smelled of charcoal and sulfur. Realization washed over Amalia and her face drained of color. She knew that smell.

Her heart sank and she dropped the basket and turned to run toward the village. This couldn't be happening. It had to be a bad dream.

"What is it?" Tomas asked as he ran after her.

"Dragons!"

A LOOK AT HALF-BLOOD DRAGON

Pirates, dragons, mermaids. A new world of mythical creatures and epic adventures await. Embark on a coming of age journey that will leave you breathless.

Time is running out for half-blood, Rowen, a lady-in-waiting to the daughter of the Dragon king. While the two princes vie for her affection, she spends her days and nights dreaming of a future free from prejudice based on her lineage. The half-blood is who she appears to be. As a prophet, she knows what the fate of the realm holds, and it's not the grand parties the kingdom is used to.

Death is on the horizon, and Rowen sees herself as its cause.

The taunts of her sleepless nights are realized when she is framed and sentenced to death for the prince's murder. For a human, there's nowhere to run and no one to turn to in a kingdom where power is tightly held by full-blooded dragon shifters.

It will take a stranger from the shadows to save Rowen from execution and reveal a truth full of terrifying potential. She must face her fears, navigate through dangerous lands, and find the courage to accept her fate, awaken her gift, and set the world on fire.

Grab your copy of this action-packed sword and sorcery adventure today!

From Chapter One

YOU'RE LUCKY TO be alive.

Those words resonated in Rowen's mind as the noose was lowered over her head and secured around her throat, scratching her delicate flesh with its coarse banding.

Not so lucky now, she thought, noting that this was the third time she'd had this nightmare in a week.

Still, she couldn't awaken. Not until she had more information. If she was going to suffer in her sleep, she was going to at least figure out the cause of the prophecy, and the result. It was all she had.

Her only gift.

Rowen coughed as her airway began to close against the ropes. Was it supposed to be so tight? It didn't matter, the wooden floor would soon disappear from beneath her and she would either break her neck from the sudden fall or suffocate.

Neither option was appealing.

Rowen looked out to the crowd of blank faces. She ignited her second sight and dug deeper into the prophecy, summoning energy from the deepest depths of her soul. She could tell the difference between a dream and a prophetic scene. It was harder to awaken from a prophecy, and for good reason. There was something she needed to see to survive, if only for a few years longer.

The people that filled the square around the gallows were nondescript. No features to their faces, and no sounds from their mouths. No movement, either. They just stood like stoic silhouettes and stared at her as she awaited her death.

A black shadow stretched across the sky, blocking the sun and dimming the courtyard. While everyone looked to the sky, Rowen's gaze peered past them, to the gates.

But, wait. Something new was happening, something Rowen had never seen in the other dreams.

Someone stood at the far end of the yard, behind the crowd, cloaked in dark gray.

The mysterious figure lifted their hand and pointed a finger right at her.

Out of the silence that filled the crisp morning air, a whisper burned her ear.

"I'm coming for you."

Then, the trap door in the floor opened and the snap of her neck woke Rowen up.

A screech erupted from her lips as she woke up, clutching at her neck. Rowen shot up from her bed. A sheen of sweat glistened on her face as she struggled to catch her breath.

The nightmares. They were relentless. But, this time, a new element had been added to her prophecy. The fates were warning her, and she needed a plan just in case the time came when she needed to escape.

Something or someone was coming for her, and she wracked her brain for who that could be.

"They know," Rowen whispered into the darkness, as she struggled to catch her breath. Escape was the only way. Her plan to restore her mother's honor would have to be abandoned.

Rowen crossed the small room and gave the sleeping girl in the bed across from hers a gentle shove.

"Brea. Wake up. I need that favor you owe me."

A quick glance out the tiny window that looked out to the back of the palace showed that the path from the castle to the gates was clear.

"Really?" Brea yawned and sat up, her white bangs falling into dark almond-shaped eyes.

"Yes." Rowen lowered herself to her knees before Brea's bed. "Please tell me you will uphold your promise."

Brea tilted her head. "I promised to help you escape if necessary. I will do what I can, Rowen."

"But, what if we are caught?"

"No one will catch us. And, if they do, we are ladies-in-waiting for the princess. We can make something up. You're a clever girl. I'm sure you can talk us out of any situation. I've seen you do it."

"You are truly the best friend I've ever had," Rowen said, giving Brea's hand a squeeze.

"You as well, dear. I will miss you. We all will."

"I'm ready," Rowen said as she shoved on her traveling frock and boots. Once her cloak was secure around her shoulders and fastened at the neck, she strapped her money purse to her thigh. It would be unwise to leave with a bag. There could be no suspicion from the palace guards.

At first, becoming a lady-in-waiting for the princess seemed like a welcome escape from her stepfather's constant scrutiny. With her new life came hope and an opportunity to restore honor to her mother's family name.

Little did she know that Withraen Castle would be significantly worse. Since childhood her prophecies had been harmless. She'd always been one step ahead of whatever fate threw at her.

Now, a mysterious being haunted her. Remaining in the palace only led Rowen one step closer to the fate of her prophecy. She had to find a way to prevent that horrible death.

Ready, Rowen watched Brea dress herself. With a nod, they left the safety of their apartment adjacent to the princess' room and entered the dark hallway of Withrae Castle's east wing.

Macana, their chaperone, would be fast asleep in her room right beside theirs. If they were quiet, they could escape unnoticed. But, they had to be quick and confident.

Brea put a finger to her lips and nodded for Rowen to follow.

Rowen chose her accomplice wisely. Brea had a gift that could save them both if caught. They crept down the stone hallway, careful not to let the soles of their boots make any noise. Clutching her opal necklace, Rowen tried to keep her face free of fear as they walked past the princess' royal guards.

Brea gave one a nod, knowing that he was sweet on her.

The stairway at the end of the hall led to the back corridors and a series of secret tunnels that they'd practiced using with the princess in case enemies stormed the castle.

"This way," Brea whispered. She led Rowen down the stairs and to a large sitting room. She hurried across the carpeted floor to the paneled wall. Rowen chewed her bottom lip as she watched Brea feel around for the hidden door. With a push, it was opened, and freedom awaited on the other end of the tunnel.

"Come."

Rowen couldn't run fast enough. They slipped through the secret door and into the dark tunnel.

"Smells of old rainwater in here," Brea said, running her hand along the slick stone.

"I don't care, as long as we make it outside."

"Do not worry, dear. You forget what I can do."

Rowen hadn't forgotten. She was just hopeful that they wouldn't need Brea's unique ability.

The large stone door at the end of the tunnel was a beacon of hope. It was so close, yet so far. They couldn't help but quicken their speed to reach it. Reaching it was a small victory. Getting out of the castle's fortified structure would be a more difficult feat.

The dark cloak of night wrapped around Rowen and Brea as they carefully wedged the door open and slipped outside. The air was humid, and the sky a dull purple shade. Soon, the sun would rise, and dragons from all over would take to the skies.

To fly. Rowen closed her eyes and wished she could do what everyone in the kingdom did without effort. To transform and outstretch her wings would be bliss. But, Rowen could not fly. No matter how hard she tried.

Rowen rubbed her arm where a dull ache lingered from a failed attempt only years ago. It was her last attempt—one where she'd nearly killed herself trying.

Together, Rowen and Brea ran across the yard for what felt like miles. Breathless, they stopped just at the bars of the gate that reached high above them and ended at the stone structure that encircled the entire castle grounds. Four gates, and this was the one with the least amount of guards as it faced the cliffs that led right into the Perilean Sea.

"The guards are about to change shifts," Brea whispered. "I can carry you over the gate and land just beyond the main road. Then, we can walk to the Gatekeeper's station. She can port you home or wherever you want to go."

Rowen narrowed her eyes as she watched four guards leave their posts as four more walked toward the front post in their armor.

"Did you save enough coins for your trip with the Gatekeeper?"

Rowen nodded. "I saved everything."

"Good," Brea said, folding her arms across her chest. "You should be able to catch a port from Withrae to Harrow with four gold zullies."

Harrow, the biggest sea port in all of Draconia, and on the border that separated the human realm from the Dragon realm.

Her home.

The wind blew at Rowen, whipping strawberry blonde hair around her face as she wrapped her pale hands around the dark bars of the gates of the palace. The cold brass was soothing, despite the nerves that burned in her belly.

Freedom.

She yearned for it above all things in the world. For as long as she could remember, she lived her life for others, with no regard for her own wishes or desires. Back at the palace, there was a silent battle she had no clue how to fight. But, beyond those gates was an even bigger battle she was too afraid to face.

The world was vast. How long before she was swallowed up by it? How long before she ended up dead?

"Are you sure about this?"

"We can do it. The guards won't even see us if you hold my hand. See?" She peeled Rowen's left hand from around the bar and held it within her own.

A warm sensation filled Rowen's body as Brea held onto her. Rowen looked from Brea's dark brown eyes and down at her hand.

"Look, I can make you vanish as well. As long as we touch," Brea said with a smile as she used her vanishing gift.

Rowen's hand and arm disappeared before her eyes, and Brea was nowhere to be seen when she looked up again.

Clever gift. She wished she had a power as great as Brea's. Still, the ability to vanish could only get them so far.

There was another world out there beyond the dragon kingdom she'd grown up in. She'd read of vast oceans and mountains, human villages and fairies. Beyond the tall brass gates was a worn path that led to the center of the kingdom of Withrae.

Once they reached the city, what then?

The free clothes, room, board, and prestige were highly coveted. Rowen's mother would call her a fool if she showed up at home before her duties had been carried out.

Rowen chewed her bottom lip, her thick brows furrowing. This wasn't the time for doubts, but her options were limited. She needed more than a few coins to make it in their world.

"What's wrong?"

Rowen sighed and pressed her forehead to the gate. "I can't go back home just yet. The Duke would just send me back by first light."

The Duke of Harrow had always hated Rowen. She was a thorn in his side since the day he married her mother. For as long as she could remember, he sent her away for every training imaginable. Languages in Summae, dancing in Dubrick, embroidery at the School for Fine Arts in Luthwig. And at eighteen, he sent her away to be a lady-in-waiting for Princess Noemie of Withraen Castle. She was merely one out of seven ladies-in-waiting, yet she was singled out at every opportunity.

Brea put a hand on Rowen's. The red shimmer of her skin reflected the moonlight. In seconds, they vanished.

"Shhh, someone is coming," Brea whispered.

Rowen tensed and peered through the bars of the gate. A rolling cart pulled by a horse with a weary-looking old man approached the gate.

"Who is it?"

"I don't know," Rowen said. "I think he's making a delivery."

"Come," Brea said. "Let's just go back. If you're worried about Prince Rickard, don't. The prince will grow weary of pursuing you before you know it. Beautiful girls come to the castle by the boatload. His eye will wander."

"It's not just that," Rowen murmured. "I'm afraid."

"Of what?"

Rowen wrung her hands. "That something terrible is going to happen to me if I stay here."

Together, they left the gate and headed back to the castle. Brea took her hand and gave it a squeeze. "Then, we try another night. We make a plan. I'll transform and you can ride on my back."

"But, I'm just thinking of how lost I am. I have nowhere to go."

"Listen to me, Rowen. My parents aren't as bad as most Dragons. If you are a friend of mine, they would take you in with open arms. Not all Dragons are prejudiced toward half-blood humans."

"Most are," Rowen quipped.

Brea wouldn't know. She was a full-blooded Dragon from high society. She couldn't have known what Rowen had seen and experienced throughout her life. In Harrow, half-bloods were more common, and she'd witnessed the cruelty to her people. Her title saved her from most of the negativity, but it was always there in the eyes of Dragons.

"Go to my home in Kabrick. I'll send you with a letter. My father and mother can find you a new station."

"I don't want that, Brea. I don't want to be a burden. I want to be free."

"You want to go to the human kingdoms, don't you?" Brea asked.

With long white hair and a hint of red scales on certain areas of her olive-colored skin, Brea was considered plain by Dragon standards. Women of beauty had a brighter shimmer to their skin, and a glow to their hair.

Like Rowen's mother.

Rowen could never be as beautiful as her mother either. Short, thin, with dull gray eyes that never shown any light, and pale skin absent of any shimmering scales, Rowen was simply different.

Maybe that's why Prince Rickard chose to pursue her.

Brea smiled at her. "I don't blame you, Rowen. But, Draconia is your home."

"It's not as if I haven't thought of finding the human kingdoms. They are my people. It would be nice to be wanted and accepted for a change."

"You are half Dragon as much as half human."

Rowen stopped on the lush landscaped evergreen grass and looked to the pale moon above. "But, your race hasn't descended from humans in thousands of years. You hate them for betraying you. For hunting you down and trying to exterminate you."

Shrugging, Brea looked into Rowen's eyes. "I don't hate anyone. That's ancient history. Nothing to do with you and me."

"I know," Rowen said with a sigh, her eyes resting on the massive castle before them. She'd only been there a few weeks, but was already twisted in a web of lies and deceit, and a plan that would elevate her family.

But, only if she succeeded.

"Maybe one day I will go find the humans."

"You can't. You can't fly or fight, or do anything that would keep you safe."

Silent, Rowen chewed her bottom lip.

I can do more than you know. Sometimes she wished she could tell Brea her secret. Even though she was the best friend she ever had, she still could not trust her with the truth of her power.

"It's too dangerous to leave the safety of the kingdom. There are beasts and monsters out there. On land and in the sea."

"There are beasts and monsters inside as well."

They paused on the cobblestone path as a large black dragon flew overhead from the city and toward the palace. It lowered itself to the ground just before the main entrance, and shifted back into a tall young man dressed in fine clothes.

Rowen took a step back, hoping that he wouldn't look back and see them. Her face paled as he seemed to sense her presence and did exactly what she hoped he wouldn't.

Prince Lawson Thorne turned and looked right at them. In the torchlight, Rowen could only make out the hints of gold in his eyes. Her heart skipped a beat as their eyes met.

Rowen took Brea's hand into her own wishing they'd been invisible when the prince arrived. "He saw us." The thought of being caught and turned in by the prince struck fear into her heart. An excuse for being out after dark is what they needed, but her mind drew a blank.

To their surprise, he simply turned away, and walked up the stairs that led into his palace.

"Well," Brea said. "Aren't we lucky?"

Rowen swallowed with a nod, curious as to why the heir to the Withraen throne didn't seem to care that they were out after curfew. "Indeed, it's all I've ever been."

Available on Amazon

BONUS STORY: A GIFTED CURSE

THICKER THAN BLOOD

PART I

ANOTHER NIGHTMARE WAS interrupted by the screams in the distant. Phoebe squeezed her eyes shut to block out the faint cries she heard echoing down the hallway.

Like a ghost, those cries haunted her.

They kept her awake for hours every night. Dark circles had formed beneath her large blue eyes. Her skin was already pale enough. Phoebe didn't need such blemishes tainting her looks.

"Phoebe," the voice screeched.

The moans of pain couldn't be ignored. Phoebe sat up as the screams vibrated down the hallway. She grumbled and glared at her door. The only traces of light in her room were that of the moonlight spilling through the maroon drapes of her large bay window.

This was the room she had grown up in.

Twenty years old and still living at home. Most college students would have jumped at the chance to move out into the dorms and fully experience college life.

Not Phoebe. She feared she'd be stuck in that old, creaky house forever. She grimaced. The bitterness of her life was almost too much to deal with.

Her parents had been dead for two years. So, there was plenty of privacy for Phoebe and her dying twin sister.

She yawned and tried to motivate herself. She needed to go and check on Tara. No one else was around to help. All things rested on Phoebe's shoulders now.

Angrily, she ripped the covers off of her body and stepped onto the cold wood floor.

"It would have been convenient to have my slippers near the bed and not beside the door," she said to herself. She found herself talking to herself more and more each day. It was all she had to keep herself sane. She could no longer stomach the sight of her sister.

"Phoebe!"

Phoebe felt her hair stand on end. Her sister's horrified cry made her suck in a cold breath. She hurried and threw her cotton robe on to keep out the icy wind that swept in through her window. The drapes danced with the howling of the wind and her head snapped toward the bedroom door.

She stood there and waited, hoping that the cries would end. She didn't want to go. The thought of what she would see churned her stomach.

"Phoebe!" Tara, her twin sister screamed.

Although Phoebe had grown used to her sister's cries of pain and sorrow, there was something new in her voice. She took off toward the door knob, disregarding the slippers that waited for her.

She swung the door open and ran into the dark hallway. Her guilt for keeping her sister in the room farthest away from hers overwhelmed her as she ran as fast as her thin legs would take her. Her footsteps pounded on the floorboards like a drum and she nearly slammed into Tara's closed door.

Phoebe snatched the door open and looked around. The darkness smothered her and the smell of blood overwhelmed her nostrils. Sweat and blood mixed to such a degree that made her nauseous.

"Tara?" Phoebe's hand searched for the light switch. Her fingertips finally found the switch and the flood of light blinded both of them. As she squinted, Phoebe's hand went to her mouth in utter terror when she saw the blood staining her sister's gown.

Tara stood there. Thin. Pale. Tara's hands were covered in the redness. She looked absolutely horrid.

Ghastly, Phoebe thought as she stared.

The cancer was merciless in its assault against her sister.

Phoebe rushed to her. She pulled the gown up from her legs. The cloth clung to Tara's legs, utterly soaked.

"It's gotten worse." Tara cried out before doubling over in pain. She squeezed her eyes shut, praying that the pain would subside.

"It...feels...like knives, stabbing me!"

Phoebe didn't know what to do. She looked over onto Tara's nightstand, seeing all of the medication bottles neatly placed and organized.

Pain killers, antibiotics, cancer meds, even vitamins. They had tried everything, and still, they could not cure Tara. Phoebe pulled the gown over Tara's head and tossed it into the hamper.

She snatched the sheets off of Tara's bed and tossed them as well. Phoebe couldn't bring herself to look into her sister's face. She knew she wouldn't be able to keep it together if she looked into her eyes. The face they shared looked so different after months of battling the greatest foe they would ever be faced with. The doctors had given up, but Phoebe had refused. She vowed to care for her sister no matter what.

Guilt filled her veins. She could have done better. She feared to admit that she had given up on her sister as well.

Tara's cold hand clamped weakly onto Phoebe's shoulder. "Phoebe. Look at me."

Her voice was hollow, distant, as though she were already fading right before her. In nothing but her blood-soaked underwear, Tara slowly sat down on the floor at the bed's side.

Phoebe finally had the courage to look straight at her. The tears choked her, rushing all at once like a broken spout. Like a baby she sobbed, seeing her sister's frail body, her thin face, and her sporadic traces of blonde hair.

They had once been the beauties of Atlanta. Beauty pageants, cheerleading competitions, boys vying for their attention. Life had been good. The future had seemed so bright.

Now, they were the twins the world had forgotten. Friends stopped showing up shortly after Tara lost her hair and her appetite for life. Only the families' old housekeeper checked on them early each morning before cleaning a house that didn't even need it anymore.

"I can't do this," Tara said weakly.

Phoebe slumped down on the floor beside her. She nodded. "I know." She felt helpless. She remembered the days when they were children. Phoebe was the older twin, the one who felt obligated to protect and watch over her sister.

Sometimes, she was certain that she felt some of Tara's pain. She would wake up in tears most nights.

"I know," Phoebe whispered.

Tara reached for her sleeping pills. "Can I?"

Phoebe pursed her lips. As she looked into Tara's dull blue eyes, she saw death staring back at her. It made her shudder.

She knew exactly what her sister meant.

Phoebe looked at the pill bottle and back at her disintegrating sister's face. Her shoulders slumped.

This wasn't the first time Tara had asked. Before, Phoebe had been vehemently against it. She had never been a quitter. She would not let Tara give up.

That girl had died months ago, when she had clung desperately to hope, to optimism. The cold, harsh, reality stood unwavering before them.

"Please, Phoebe." Tara shook the bottle before her. The clink of pills filled the silence of that stifling room.

Phoebe looked away.

"I can't do this anymore! We tried it your way, and we failed!" she cried, mucous dripping from her nose. She wiped her face of the salty tears.

"Just let me go!"

Phoebe shook with her sister's words. The echo bounced off the bare walls. She stared blankly.

Her mouth opened to protest. Nothing came out.

She closed her mouth and swallowed. Her throat felt dry.

Tara's didn't blink. She waited.

Phoebe did something she hadn't expected.

She nodded.

Tara gasped when Phoebe took the bottle from her sister's hands and twisted the top off.

Phoebe poured about a quarter of the bottle into Tara's tiny hand. She handed her the bottle of water that sat beside the lamp on the nightstand.

Tara stared at her for a moment, sucking her tears up. "Thank you, Phoebe," she said and poured the handful into her mouth. She gulped down half the bottle of water.

To Tara's surprise, Phoebe poured the remaining contents of the bottle into her own mouth. And wrenched the water bottle from Tara's hand.

"I'm coming with you!" Phoebe said, her voice cracking after she swallowed the pills.

Phoebe didn't think it was even possible for

Tara's face to flush even more. Like looking into a mirror they stared at each other.

Tara nodded and hugged her sister close. All Phoebe felt were bones. Tara was so cold.

"You didn't have to do that," Tara said between sobs.

Phoebe sniffled. "What else is there for me?

I've been thinking about it for a while now. I won't let you go on this journey alone. I will always be by your side…" Phoebe held Tara's hand. Her voice trailed as her heavy eyelids closed.

PART II

HER FEET WERE wet. She was barefoot and cold. The wind whipped her long blonde hair around her face and the sound of rushing water was deafeningly loud in her ears.

Phoebe opened her eyes. Something wasn't right. Her heart sped. She saw nothing but darkness. She started to hyperventilate as she touched her eyelids to make sure that her eyes were indeed open.

She flinched when she felt her wet eyeball. A cry of panic escaped her lips. Everywhere she turned there was nothing but a thick black film over her eyes. She ripped at her eyes until they were raw and screamed in frustration.

"Why is this happening?" Phoebe cried. "Can I wake up now? Please?" Her voice sounded tiny and weak, as though she stood in an open field.

"Phoebe!"

Phoebe paused. Her ears perked up. She tilted her head to where she heard the voice. It sounded like Tara.

"Tara?"

Phoebe heard water splash as Tara ran to her.

"You're here!" Tara squealed excitedly.

Phoebe was confused by her sister's enthusiasm. "Where is here?" she asked hesitantly. She wasn't sure she wanted to know. A warning tugged at her stomach, making her feel anxious and ill.

She wanted to see Tara's face. She wanted to see where they were. A breeze swept through and nearly knocked her to her feet.

Tara giggled, hugging her. Phoebe blinding reached out and returned the hug. "I don't know! But it's beautiful!" Tara replied. "My god. It's the most beautiful place I've ever seen."

Phoebe clung to her sister, afraid that if she moved she might fall into a bottomless pit. Her sister's presence only mildly calmed her anxiety.

"What is beautiful, Tara?" Phoebe gripped her sister's shoulders. "There's nothing here but black darkness and shadows!"

"What are you babbling about?" Tara chimed. "It's amazing. There's the most beautiful blue sky without a cloud in sight! The water is so crystalline that I can see silver fish swimming beneath the waterfall. The grass is so green it looks like Mr. Boswell's yard. You know the one he pays hundreds of dollars getting treated with fertilizers and stuff…"

"Stop it!" Phoebe shouted, cutting her sister off.

There was silence.

"Why?" Tara asked, sounding disappointed.

"Because you're making it all up Tara! There's nothing here!" She was angry. Jealous. She wanted to see what Tara saw. Why did she have to be blind?

"You're wrong, Phoebe," she paused. There was silence as Tara observed her sister's face. Phoebe's eyes were glossy as if a film covered them.

Tara scrunched up her nose as she waved her hand before Phoebe's eyes. "You really can't see it, can you?"

Phoebe nodded. "I think I've gone blind, Tara." The more she tried to see around her, the more frantic she became. "I can't see anything."

"Shh," Tara said and stopped to listen. "Oh, Phoebe! They're calling us, singing to us," she exclaimed grabbing Phoebe's hand. "Let's go!"

Phoebe didn't have a chance to protest as her sister pulled her along too quickly for her comfort. "I can't see, Tara! Slow down before I fall!"

"Trust me!" Tara shouted back. Her sweet voice was light and full of happiness that Phoebe hadn't heard in years.

Her happiness was enough to silence her into submission. She ran as fast as she could, trying to stay with Tara. She clutched her tiny hand like it was a lifesaver as if she might drown if she let go.

"Ok," she breathed. She trusted her sister. It was all she had left.

Tara began to sing as she ran, along to whatever melody she heard, but Phoebe heard nothing but her sister's voice. Being unable to see was unnerving. Being unable to hear what her sister heard was frightening.

Phoebe's stomach was in knots. She wanted to vomit.

Tiny rocks stung the soles of her feet as they flew through what felt like winding roads. The crisp air swooshed past her ears. Phoebe had to know where they were. She couldn't live an eternity, blind to the beauty Tara claimed surrounded them.

Her stomach lurched forward when they stopped abruptly. She knew they were at a cliff, she heard the stones fall off the edge as they skidded to a stop. The silence that followed was unbearable.

"They sing," Tara explained, her voice full of awe. She gave Phoebe's hand a squeeze.

"Do they?" Phoebe was annoyed. She felt cold. She was afraid. "And who are they?"

Tara hugged her tight. She buried her face in

Phoebe's neck. Phoebe felt Tara's warm tears run down her skin. "What's wrong?" Phoebe asked as her fear intensified.

"Oh, Phoebe," Tara whispered.

"What is it?" Phoebe's eyes widened. Her sister's tone was unnerving.

"You can't cross here Phoebe," she sobbed.

"You're not supposed to be here!"

Phoebe pulled back. "Hold on a second," she said quickly. "What are you talking about?" She suddenly felt like she was being watched by more than her sister.

"Who's singing, Tara? Tell me!" She was on the brink of hysterics. She could feel eyes on her, all around, and it made her skin crawl with terror.

What was this mysterious place?

Tara let go of her hand and Phoebe felt an emptiness that terrified her. She felt naked and alone.

"They sing," she heard Tara say softly, sucking up her tears. "Just for me."

Phoebe reached out for her sister and felt her face. Her skin was warm and soft. Phoebe's hands were the cold ones this time. She felt absolutely frigid.

Tara caught her hand and kissed it. Phoebe felt her heart pause. Then, Tara pushed her off the cliff, into the abyss that she was sure she would soon meet. Tara's voice trailed after her.

"Go back, Phoebe. Go home!"

PART III

PHOEBE'S EYES POPPED open with such a pain as she'd never felt. All she saw was light. Brighter than she'd ever experienced in her entire life. She tried to scream, but something was lodged in her throat.

Phoebe started to panic. The pain was unbearable.

She felt as though her entire stomach was being forced up her throat, tugged by something foreign, something devoid of any pity for her cries of pain.

Hands held her down, restraining her arms and legs as she bucked, keeping her head down and tilted. Her eyes stung with tears and she felt violated by the hands.

Why was that light so bright? She wondered.

Had she finally reached the end? Was this it?

Her vision started to clear and she stared up at the nurses and the doctor who pumped away at her stomach, trying to purge her stomach of its contents.

Her heart leaped with joy as realization flooded her. Even

through the pain, she was glad to be alive. Glad for her second chance.

Still, Tara's singing lingered in her mind.

PART IV
THE GALLOWAY LAKE

TANYA'S BODY CRASHED into the icy lake. It was a violent awakening.

Like a slap in the face, her mind was jolted by the impact.

Dark brown eyes popped open to the rush of the murky water. Her body tightened at the chill of it. It felt like a thousand knives pricking her exposed flesh.

Without light to see her surroundings, she panicked and kicked. She tried to keep her head above the water, to see a shred of hope, but the handcuffs that bound her hands behind her back made every movement difficult.

Death was not an option.

Tanya wouldn't allow it. Even after days of torture, she never gave up her will to live. Her body and mind would be forever bruised by the abuse she suffered. Water filled every orifice as her head sunk again. The darkness terrified her. Her fear of drowning and what lurked deep in the lake was being realized.

The handcuffs were her only obstacle. She was an avid swimmer and had won countless medals and awards for her skill.

She might survive if she could get free. Little did her kidnapper know, but Tanya was double jointed. She squeezed her hands very tight and mashed her fingers together until the bone in her thumb tucked inward.

Tanya pursed her lips together and tried to clear her thoughts. Her lungs burned and yet she had to concentrate. After a moment of suffocating agony, her right hand slipped out of the metal handcuffs.

Tanya sprang into action and swam to the surface as quickly as her fatigued body would take her. Her lungs swelled with the air that entered when her head broke the surface. Tanya choked and coughed in ragged fits. Her throat burned from the water she had swallowed.

All was quiet around her. Tanya sucked in a breath and felt her fear rise. She looked around in desperation. She pulled her black hair out of her eyes. Everything was calm and still. She could see her breath puff into the air before her. Tiny lanterns hung from the bridge. Tanya knew where she was.

This was the bridge that led to the Galloway
Plantation. The lanterns lit the way to the shore.

She had to reach dry land. The fact that she was naked in the frosty air of made it dire for her to get out of the water.

Tanya swam as hard as she could. She reached the shore and collapsed onto the rocky ground.

Pebbles and rocks embedded into her arms and legs.

She cried out in both joy and pain. Her head crashed into the mud and she didn't care. Her eyes closed and she nearly passed out again from days of malnutrition and exhaustion. She wondered if he knew she was still alive when he tossed her over the bridge.

Tanya had to be strong. She had to stay focused. Tanya was an athlete. Her training was all that she had left.

Pain was weakness. Tanya refused to be weak.

The forest was a mass of black shadows that reached the lake's shore, the branches of the trees hung over the water like a canopy.

Tanya looked to the forest and felt her body tense. There was nothing but a silent darkness all around her, and the forest went deeper and deeper, making her dizzy as she tried to make out what shadows lingered.

It reminded her of the days when she would stare into the woods in her parents back yard and imagine she'd seen goblins watching her from the trees.

Tanya swallowed hard and rubbed the gooseflesh in her arms. She winced. The gashes were still bleeding. Tanya glanced down at the blood on her hands and felt her lips quiver. She could still remember the sting of the ropes that had cut into her flesh.

She had hung like a pig ready to be butchered for so long that the ropes had dug deep, and all of the blood in her body had traveled down to her head.

Tanya squeezed her eyes shut and tried to block out the memories. She blew into her hands to warm them. It was useless. Her hands had lost all feeling already.

Tanya fought her weariness and shivered as she crawled to her feet.

"Tanya, you can do this." She tried to motivate herself, but the sound of her voice, so fragile and cracked made her weep.

She couldn't believe she had let such a thing happen to her. She had always been careful. Her mother had always warned her. The day Tanya had left for college, her mother had told her to be aware of her surroundings.

"Always look around to make sure no one followed you when you're alone. Never get in your car without checking the back seat first. Never go alone to a party or club. Always watch your drink. Call mommy if you need a ride home. Just be aware, Tanya."

But I was aware! Tanya screamed in her head.

She missed her mother's voice more than anything.

For days she had gone over and over what had gone wrong.

Tanya always checked her surroundings. She was cognizant of who was around and watching her.

Still, Tanya couldn't have prepared for what had happened. He bragged to her about how meticulous he was. He had watched her for years. He knew every detail of her schedule. This had been planned for a while now.

So, one night, he finally came to her. The man in the black mask stole her from the comfort of her own bed.

Tanya shook her head, as though trying to purge herself of the memories. She didn't want to remember anything now. All she could think was that she was so cold, hungry, and so tired.

The forest seemed to reach out to her as she ran from it. Her heart beat faster. She heard rustling in the trees and nearly cried out in terror.

She glanced back over her shoulder and saw nothing in the bushes and trees that hung with gray

Spanish moss.

Tanya couldn't think straight. Every thought was of horrible possibilities. Maybe someone was practicing voodoo back there in those woods.

Maybe the man in the black mask was watching her. Perhaps this was a game, and he was ready to capture her again. It wasn't too far-fetched.

Tanya cringed. He did love his games. He certainly enjoyed watching her suffer.

Tanya heard something crunch behind her, and despite a sore ankle, she ran as fast as she could to the bridge. The fear ignited such an adrenaline rush that she was able to climb the side of the hill that led to the street.

The mud and dirt smeared onto her pale hands as she fought her way to the pavement.

It was a two-lane street, one that not many people drove down because it led to the old Galloway Plantation. She figured that was the closest place for her to seek help. Tanya felt somewhat safer once her feet touched the cold, wet, asphalt.

Her stomach churned and her face was still sore. Tanya couldn't wait for warmth. Her skin was tight. She couldn't slow her pace.

She wasn't sure where she obtained such vitality, but she suspected it was the fear that something still watched her from the forest that sat on either side of the road.

Tanya gulped. She couldn't stifle the tears. She could have easily curled into a ball and fallen into a hypothermic slumber, but she was not a quitter.

"Treat this like a race Tanya, you can do it," she told herself.

Her eyes widened with hope when she finally saw lights in the distance. They were dim. Only the pale gold lanterns lit the gate to the estate. She was praying that someone was home.

Then, she realized that the large, shiny black gate was closed and locked. She banged every number on the call box. She shivered.

Tanya didn't have much time. She was frantic. She beat the silver box with her numb hand until she was dizzy.

PART V

"DADDY?" AVA SAT up from her place on the floor. She put the jumbo crayon she had been using down on the yellow construction paper and stood.

"Yeah?" her father asked, not looking up from the book he read.

"What's that noise? Is someone trying to get in?" Ava listened to the loud beeping that came from a system of equipment that sat on the desk.

"Oh. That again." He closed his book and sat up in his chair. He looked at the security monitor and turned the call box off. The loud beeping ceased.

Ava's eyes widened and she tilted her head to listen. She heard faint wailing. She suddenly wished she was at home with his mother, safe in her warm bed.

She didn't like the security room her father worked in. She didn't like that big plantation house either. It frightened her.

"Come here. Sit with daddy for a second. "Her father motioned for her to sit on his lap.

Ava did so quickly. Someone was still crying.

"Daddy!" She jumped into her father's lap, clutching her father's neck.

"Oh, Ava, I'm sorry. I should have just got a babysitter tonight." He smoothed the girl's hair, trying to calm her.

"What is that Daddy? Why don't you go help that girl?" Ava pulled back to look into his eyes. "She's not real Ava. There's nothing I can do."

Ava brows furrowed. "What do you mean, she's not real?"

He sighed. "You see Ava, look at this screen."

Ava turned, looking at the assortment of screens above the desk. He pointed to the screen that monitored the front gate.

Ava nodded. "Yes, I see."

"OK, good. Daddy watches over this house every night. And every night this happens... but no one is there."

Ava tilted her head. She didn't take her eyes off of that screen. She turned back to face her father.

"What do you mean? Why don't you help her daddy?"

He was taken aback by his daughter's exasperation. He ran his fingers through his graying hair.

"Help who?" He looked at the screen and shook his head. "Ava," he pointed again, at the large gate. "See? No one is there. Something is wrong with the equipment here. I used to go check, but no one is ever outside at the gate."

Ava stared at the screen. The wind howled outside, but it didn't drown out the naked girls screams.

"See? Nothing."

Ava frowned at him. "Why are you joking daddy? Help her!"

His shoulders slumped and he sighed. The girl just didn't understand. "Ava, go draw me another picture or something." He was done trying to explain such things to a child. "There's no one there, and that's all there is to it.

Ava didn't budge. Her little finger pressed the screen. "But I see her daddy! I see her!"

Her father didn't say anything. He stared at Ava, then at the screen, and gulped. He felt cold and very exposed as if someone was watching him.

He'd never feared that job before, but something about Ava's exclamation made his stomach churn with dread.

He stared at the screen. The black gate stood in a cloud of fog. The soft lights cast a glow around it and all he saw were the vines that wrapped around the bars.

He scratched his chin and peered closer. He couldn't shake the feeling that something was wrong. There were always stories of ghosts lingering near the plantation, but he'd never put much credit to the rumors.

Now...he wasn't so sure. For years he had dealt with strange sounds and electrical malfunctions.

"Foolishness Ava, it's time for you to go to bed." He spoke those words, but couldn't take his eyes off of the screen. He motioned behind him as he studied the image and for just a second, he thought he saw a shadow, being swept away by the wind.

His heart thumped. "Get in your sleeping bag and go to sleep."

Ava frowned at him but didn't argue. She felt bad for that girl. Ava went to bed that night with the girl with the black hair's face embedded into her mind.

TANYA'S BODY CRASHED into the icy lake. It was a violent awakening. Like a slap in the face, her mind was jolted by the impact. Her eyes popped open to the rush of the murky water.

THE LAST OF THE JINN

MALAH RUMMAGED THROUGH the dead guard's clothing. Sweat dripped from her forehead onto his chest as the heat of the room gained intensity. With each droplet of sweat, his bare-chested skin sizzled.

Malah grew dizzy and despite the heat felt a debilitating coldness crawl under her skin as her hand searched the last pocket.

Nothing.

She pulled her dagger from the guard's head and wiped it clean on the bottom of her nightgown. Her eyes scanned the corridor. Four dead Parthan soldiers lie on the stone floor. None of them had an antidote for whatever poison the clerics had given her. Her full belly churned. She pressed her hand to her belly and closed her eyes with a sigh. Life stirred beneath her palm.

Two innocent lives.

The Parthans may be strong and powerful, but her gifts gave her an advantage, even if Dwy and his Cleric did weaken her.

The Reen guards that patrolled the exit would not be so easy to kill. They were larger, stronger, and composed of stone. Malah wished that they'd never been created. They had kept her prisoner for too long.

Malah opened her eyes and breathed in deeply. Within moments, cold air made her golden skin tighten and her toes and fingers numb. Her arms raised and she squeezed her eyes closed as she fed power to the air around her. She peeked through one of her eyelids to see the stone guards turn from brown, to gray.

Frozen, they would not give her any trouble for the next few minutes.

Minutes. That's all she had.

Whispers filled her head as she ran down the chilly corridor. The dark didn't bother her, but the voices did. They'd never allow her to escape. Not when the entire planet needed her for its survival.

Malah didn't care about them anymore. She wanted to go home. If she could rid their poisons from her body, she could finally think straight again.

She cursed herself for being so stupid. Why had she allowed herself to fall in love? She should have known better. Love never ended well. Hadn't she seen the results of such a foolish emotion enough times before? Why hadn't she learned from her ancestors?

Love is a curse, Malah thought with a bitter grimace. She tried to shove Dwy's black eyes from her mind. His touch used to be so gentle. The heartbreak hurt more than the betrayal.

Malah wrung her hands. The gray guards slept upright, like statues, their hands formed into daggers, but kept inside the metallic scabbards at their sides. It looked like they simply had their hands in their pockets, but she knew better. She only hoped they wouldn't be activated before she could escape.

"One, two, three, four," she chanted into her cold hands. Her power was weak. Her heart seemed to shake inside her chest.

She had neglected her practice for far too long. She rubbed her hands together and poured out a tiny burst of power. "Yolie! Please, come forth!"

A small light formed in the palm of her hand.

Malah smiled. Her heart thumped, but this time, it was with

hope. Perhaps her skills weren't too rusty after all.

The light turned into a ball. She puckered her golden lips and kissed it. The ball of light began to take the form of a tiny figure. The figure uncurled itself. A pop of lightning slammed into the figure and the sound of bells filled Malah's ears.

"Sweet Blessings," Malah breathed with relief. She dared to let a smile appear on her lips. *When was the last time I smiled*, she wondered. She pursed her lips and shook her head. *No time for reminiscing.*

Yolie's bright smile warmed her heart she rested on her knees. Like a doll, Malah's favorite Blessing had returned. After years of being unable to call upon her, they were once again reunited.

Malah could have jumped for joy. Instead, she hid in a corner, with her back against the cold stone wall. She watched the tiny person look up at her with large red eyes that sparkled like rubies. Then, it tugged at its black hair, making it longer and longer, until the curling locks could be coiled around its body like a dress.

"Blessed One," the creature called. She stood in Malah's hand and looked around. "Where are we this time?"

Malah closed her eyes and sighed. She rested her head against the wall and shrugged. "Yolie, we are in big trouble. We are in Partha."

Yolie's big eyes widened. "No, Blessed One. We have to get out of here! This is not one of ours!"

"That's why I summoned you. I need your help."

Yolie nodded but pursed her thin lips. "But Blessed One, what do you need me to do?" She sprouted red wings and flew from Malah's golden hand to hover just inches from Malah's face.

Malah's gaze lifted to the open air ceiling. The passing sky beckoned to her. The clouds seemed to float and dance and she remembered what it felt like to be free. Free to fly with her family. She felt a stab in her heart as she realized that she would never fly with them again. She was the last, but she would not let that stop her.

"How did you get here, Blessed One?" Yolie asked. "We are far from home."

Malah sighed. She gave Yolie a sheepish look from beneath her golden bangs. "I was curious. I wanted to see what this new race looked like."

Yolie frowned. "Why? I don't understand."

Malah shook her head. "It isn't important. I need you to fly me out of here."

Yolie clapped her hands. "Oh yes! Yes! I can do it! Let's go home! Let's play together again. I do miss our games, Blessed One."

Malah glanced back. It was still quiet in the temple. She might have a chance. Her hands shook. She looked down at them and nearly wept. Blood covered her small golden hands. It had seeped into the crevices of her palm and dried to a dry, sticky, paste. She'd never had to kill anyone before. She'd never had a reason to.

Now, nine dead guards and a cleric would haunt her dreams for all eternity. Even if they deserved their fate, the guilt would never fade.

"Good," Malah said and stepped back to give Yolie room. "Go on. Shift."

Yolie made a face. "You forget, Blessed One. I need more of your blessing."

Malah sighed. She had forgotten. Her head was so full of fuzzy thoughts that she could barely think straight. She was losing time. The poison was too strong. Her vision blurred, but she nodded and held a palm out for Yolie to sit in. "Okay, quickly."

Yolie flew into Malah's hand and bowed on her knees.

Gold light filled the room as Malah ignited her blessing. Her golden body levitated as she breathed soft words into her palm. "I give you love. I give you light. I give you the power to Shift and take flight."

Yolie opened her eyes and smiled. "That was beautiful, Blessed One. Thank you."

Malah fell to her knees and hung her head, drained. "You deserve every blessing, Yolie. Now please hurry."

Yolie nodded quickly and flew into the air. She stretched her red wings and flexed her dangling legs. Her hair unwrapped from around her body and floated around her as she Shifted. Red feathers started to grow all over her pale naked flesh. Her face was covered, and her hair continued to float. Like a giant bird, Yolie's nose became a red beak and her eyes grew larger. She bowed to Malah.

"Climb on, Blessed One."

Malah leaped into the air with grace and landed onto Yolie's smooth back. She pressed her face to Yolie's feathers and held onto her neck.

"Take me home, Yolie," Malah whispered. "They have hurt me, and I need to recharge."

Yolie's body vibrated as she purred. "Oh Blessed One. Yolie told you to be careful. Yolie is always right."

Malah squeezed her eyes shut. Tears stung her eyes and she wiped them on Yolie's smooth back. Life grew inside of her. Such a miracle was true power. Even as a child when Malah went through training, she never imagined she'd be able to do something so incredible.

Despite the pain of being betrayed by her husband, she was escaping, with their unborn children. The last hope for the Jinn.

A loud explosion made Malah gasp. Shards of green magic shot out towards her. Something clamped around her neck and yanked her from Yolie's back.

Malah screamed for her friend as she was pulled from the air and sent crashing to the hard floor. Yolie fought back and was stabbed by the tip of a red bone spear. Her bird-like screech ripped through the air, sending waves of vibrations throughout the entire room.

Malah had to act quickly. She reached out and created a glowing door that hovered in the air. She could never live with the guilt of a friend's death, and so, she banished her. "Away with you!" she cried.

Yolie obeyed, as always. She nodded. Her white body flickered and faded into the cold air. Her essence seeped into the doorway and the door vanished.

Malah wiped the blood from her face and glared at the clerics in red cloaks that surrounded her. Protecting the clerics were Parthan soldiers with their bone spears.

Vornid peered down at her from beneath his hood. He reached a hand to Malah's face and grabbed her by her soft cheeks.

Malah squirmed as the abnormally tall cleric lifted her from the ground. She dangled before him like a child as his black eyes bore into hers. The grip he had on her neck made her sick. She trembled. He wanted to crush her throat, but such a thing would ruin them all. As much as he hated her.

The entire Parthan race needed her.

"Who said that you could go anywhere, *Blessed* One?"

Malah felt a hot tear trail from her eye and down her cheek. Vornid watched the tear as it fell to his gloved hand. He raised a brow as it burnt through the black fabric.

His eyes flickered up to hers, the wrinkles in his forehead deepening as his brows furrowed. Malah could see much knowledge in his eyes. Too much knowledge, and still not enough.

"I will kill you, Vornid. You know this," Malah said after sucking in a breath. "It is a promise."

Vornid's dry gray lips curled into a grin. She could smell milk on his breath. The milk of a nursing mother. It turned her stomach.

"No, you won't," he whispered.

Malah cried out as he put his other hand on the top of her head, nearly crushing her skull. Heat filled her head and her body shook while Vornid held her. She had no choice. At this time, Vornid was more powerful than her. Too much poison filled her veins.

Malah fought it, with all of her strength, but within seconds she met the eerie black of her own mind.

MALAH NEVER LIKED being inside her own mind. This time was no exception.

This time was torture.

While her body was paralyzed, her mind was free to witness it all. The Clerics injected her with more of their special poisons. The thick blue liquid filled her veins and forced her into a coma that was deep enough to make her sleep through the birth of her twin daughters.

Malah never even imagined actually birthing children. She'd never had to. She'd always had her Blessings to keep her company. If only she could call upon Yolie. But Yolie could not come unless called.

She'd watched, from outside of her body, as her beautiful girls were taken from her stomach and ushered away. She'd wept and screamed, and no one had heard her. She'd pleaded with Dwy. She'd begged him to forgive her, let her have another chance at being a dutiful wife, and to, please, wake her up. She had been foolish, like a child. Curiosity got her tricked and captured.

Of course, no one could see her. The people of this land could not leave their bodies like the Jinn. And there were no more real Jinn. She was the last, and that is why they lured her with love and kept her prisoner.

She wondered if Dwy ever truly loved her. He'd been so gentle in the beginning.

Malah knew the truth. The Parthans needed her for this last task. That was when the harsh reality truly hit her. She was merely a vessel. A treasure used to make their race more powerful.

Malah retreated to the corner of her quarters and curled into a ball, and waited for someone to finally awaken her.

The moment she opened her eyes and breathed fresh air again didn't come until four years had passed.

Dwy stood beside her cot. His black eyes were fixed on hers. He touched her face.

"Dwy," she croaked.

He reached over and handed her a cup of red liquid.

Gremmina. A drink from her homeland's enchanted springs.

Malah snatched the cup from him. She wondered how he had got his hands on the precious fluid as she drank the pungent substance down. She watched him with wide eyes as she hurried to drink every drop. When the cup was empty, she shot to her feet. She balled her fists up and glared at him.

"You stupid creature," she said. "You do know that Gremmina gives me enough strength to kill all of you. I could crush this palace into a pile of rubble."

Footsteps drew her attention. Her glare shot to Vorrid. He came from the archway that led to her study room. He was cloaked as always and carried a large pitcher of the Gremmina.

Malah stepped back. "It isn't Gremmina? Is it?" Even as she asked the question she knew the answer. It had to be Gremmina. She could feel its effects. But why would her enemy give her such a valuable weapon?

Vorrid nodded. He poured more into the cup. "It is, Blessed One."

Malah raised a brow. "You sound as if you mean it now. And yet, you do not pay homage." Her hands were held ready to summon all manners of creatures to aid her in killing them both. One thought stopped her. She had two girls somewhere in the palace that she would not leave without.

To her surprise, they both bowed to her.

Malah swallowed. "What are you up to?"

Vorrid and Dwy shared a look. Dwy was king. Vorrid was his

personal cleric, the most powerful sorcerer in Partha. But while at her optimum strength, Malah did not fear anyone or anything. She would never let her guard down again.

"Shall I show her?" Vorrid asked from his knees. When Dwy nodded, Vorrid stood and turned to walk across the large stone room to the tall window that stretched from the high ceiling to the granite floor. Malah watched him.

Her heart beat loudly in her ears. She only wanted her daughters, Keema and Livie. Dwy had at least told her about their daughters' triumphs and milestones during her long slumber. She wondered if he knew that she had seen it all. Even if her physical body was at rest, her mind could still work wonders. She had watched them grow but from a painful distance.

When Vorrid opened the black shutters, Malah slumped to her knees. Her hand shot to cover her mouth as she stared at the scene outside her bedroom window. The once lush and beautiful land of Partha was a black, desolate wasteland.

Malah stared at the scene with wide, horrified eyes. When she finally found her voice she stuttered, "What happened?"

Vorrid sat in a stone chair at her breakfast table beneath the window. He removed his cloak's hood and ran his long, thin fingers through his silver and black hair. He sighed.

"Sire," he began. "You should tell her."

Dwy took a deep breath. He was a big Parthan, with broad shoulders and muscles that bulged. He towered over her by two feet and now he looked small to her. He looked afraid.

That made Malah afraid. And Malah had rarely ever felt fear.

"You did this, Blessed One."

Malah came to her feet. Her jaw hung slack. "What?"

Vorrid nodded. "It is true. As you slept, you destroyed our land. We want you to forgive us, and leave."

Malah's hands balled into fists. She hadn't realized what she had done during her slumber, she'd been so focused on her children. She hadn't paid attention to what the dark places in her mind were doing to the world outside.

An almost evil grin came to her lips. "You should have listened to me. I told you who and what I was, and you tricked me. I may have been too young to learn everything from the other Jinn before they vanished, but your treachery has taught me a great lesson." Her palms opened. "I hope I taught you something as well."

She breathed into both of her palms and summoned two giants to restrain her husband and his cleric. The cleric and the king didn't even fight back. They were docile, defeated.

She raised a hand and the door burst open. Freedom. She darted like lightning through the palace.

"Keema! Livie!" she shouted at the top of her lungs until she was hoarse. She swept past palace servants too quickly for them to even catch a glimpse of her. When at full power, a Jinn was unstoppable. The Parthans knew that now. They'd never doubt again true power.

Her hair flew behind her as she searched for her children. Hate and rage boiled inside of her. The Parthans would pay.

They already had. She'd made sure of that. She didn't pause when she saw that there weren't any guards around to stop her. All she passed as she searched the labyrinth of hallways were frightened servants and clerics who bowed to their statues and begged for forgiveness and aid in their last hours. The sight almost made Malah feel bad for them.

Almost.

She finally sensed them, her babies. She could smell their sweet golden hair that was nearly the same shade as her own. Her little beauties would rule worlds once she took them from this place. She pushed through the double doors that led into the temple. She slowed down at the sight of rows upon rows of Parthan citizens and clerics bowed to the worship platform at the end of the red and black room.

Malah's eyes went down the aisle. She froze when she finally saw them. Malah's golden face turned red as she saw the bodies of her daughters laid on a pyre before the god Huji, a large snake-like statue of gold. To the bitter end, they remained pagans.

Her scream remained trapped in her throat. She felt every vein pulse with rage as black tears poured from her eyes. She couldn't breathe. She couldn't speak.

Their tiny bodies were impaled and now waited to be burned. Finally, Malah found her voice, and with a scream, she called every creature she'd ever learned about as a child in the temples. She called them forth with one breath of power. Chaos erupted in the palace, but Malah was numb to it all. Her spawn killed everyone in sight as she slowly walked over to the golden pyre. She stroked her daughter's golden hair and buried her face in the silken strands.

The black tears fell down her cheeks as she sobbed like a baby. She'd never had a chance to hold them. Not in real life. Only in her dreams.

A familiar whistle made her pause.

"Yolie?" she whispered.

"Blessed One! We can go now! Let's go!"

Malah turned to her. She almost smiled at her friend's beauty. She glowed in the midst of such darkness. Behind Yolie was a massacre. Her creatures had killed everyone in sight and now, they all bowed to her, silent and waiting for a command.

Malah pulled her children free of the piles and cradled their bodies into either side of her as she sat on the bottom step of the worship platform.

Yolie looked confused. "Who are they?"

Malah wiped tears from her eyes and sucked in a painful breath. The tears wouldn't stop. She could barely talk.

"They are mine."

Yolie flew over to her. She landed on Malah's knee and looked at the girls. "Yours?"

Malah nodded. "Mine. I don't even want to think of what they could have been."

Yolie lifted herself off of Malah's knee and flew before her face. Her small face was full of innocence and purity that Malah almost felt at peace just by looking at her.

"They could have been true gods, like you," Yolie said.

Malah turned away. The shame was too much to handle.

"Right, Blessed One?"

Malah simply nodded. She didn't want to admit that she had failed not only her people on her planet but her children.

Yolie flew closer and kissed the tip of her nose. "Do not cry, Blessed One," she said.

Malah sighed and tried to will away the tormenting pain in her heart.

"We can make another world," Yolie said. "It wasn't so hard the first time. I remember when we started that world centuries ago. Since then we've become much better, right?"

Malah felt even deeper sorrow at her first failed world.

"Can't you breathe life back into their bodies?" Yolie asked.

Malah shook her head. She looked down at her children. Their souls were already gone. Malah stroked their hair.

Out of the corner of her eye, she saw a baby mouse skitter across the floor, the last surviving creature of her world. Yolie caught the tiny, gray creature, cradled it in her own small hand.

"Life is such a fragile thing," she said, before letting the creature go free.

Malah gently laid her children down, kissed their foreheads, and reached a hand out for Yolie to rest in. Yes, so fragile, but together, they would give life one last try. They would make one more world. Malah vowed that if they failed again, then she would simply rest.

She'd rest until the pain faded. She'd never fall in love with her creations again.

BONUS STORY: AWAKENED

INTRODUCTION

One line blurb: A young witch betrays her darkest secret and risks her crown, life, and soul for the love of a human.

CHAPTER 1

Cambridgeshire, England

CHAPTER 2

WILLA RACED THROUGH her garden to the road. After an afternoon of napping on a blanket just beside the pond, she'd almost missed the moment she'd been awaiting all day. The post was on its way, and she would die if she didn't receive an invitation from the Dargaard family. At seventeen, this would be her last year of innocence. Her last year to enjoy a life of her own design.

Destiny awaited.

Just not today.

Today, she just wanted to be a young lady, fuss over what elaborate gown she would wear, and try her charms on the young Master Kristoff Dargaard.

Not the intended queen of the Grand Elite Casters.

A witch.

A giggle escaped her lips as she skidded to a stop, right before the post man. The sun reflected off of his bifocals, making his blue eyes look terribly big.

"Good day, Mr. Fulton," Willa said with a slight curtsy.

Mr. Fulton cleared his throat and gave a deep bow. "Good day to you, Miss Avery."

"Do you have something for me?" Willa's eyes peered at his brown satchel, hoping to catch a letter or parcel with her name on it.

"Hmmm," Mr. Fulton said, rummaging through his bag. "I don't believe I saw anything for you today."

Shoulders slumping, Willa sucked her teeth. "It can't be," she said, leaving the plush grass of her family's land, to stand on the hard-packed dirt road that led to town. Forgetting decorum, she stood right before Mr. Fulton and dug her hands into the bag.

Instead of scolding her, he chuckled and took off his cap. "All right! All right," he said and pulled a cream-colored envelope with the Dargaard seal.

"You scoundrel!"

Willa took the envelope, a smile spreading from ear-to-ear and ran back toward the manor. She couldn't get to her mother and father fast enough to share the great news. Dreams of securing Kristoff as a suitor had been her mother's plan since the day his family moved to their village from Norway. Having such exotic neighbors was the talk of the town. Not to mention the Dargaards were reported to be the wealthiest family in theirs and the five surrounding counties.

That meant little to Willa. All she cared about was how charming, and attractive the young lord was.

"You're welcome," Mr. Fulton shouted after her with a laugh.

Looking over her shoulder, Willa shouted back. "Thank you!" She gathered her skirts in her hand and quickened her speed. Dark tightly-wound curls bounced around her face as she made her way to the front entrance.

The instant she stepped into the doorway, and enter the vaulted foyer, her mother called her name.

"Willa," she said, her voice echoing off of the walls and high ceiling.

Face draining of color, Willa turned to her mother. Something in her voice told Willa that something was wrong.

Very wrong.

"Yes," Willa asked, catching her breath. She folded her arms behind her back, hiding the invitation.

Lady Anna Avery looked Willa over and pursed her pert pink lips. Without a line of age on her face, most just believed that Lady Anna had a secret cream or diet. They'd never guess that Casters simply aged slower than most humans.

Willa, on the other hand, would stop aging completely at eighteen.

The thought alone both intrigued and frightened her. Not all Casters were granted immortality. So, she knew that one day she would have to say goodbye to her unfortunate loved ones.

Squeezing her eyes shut, she willed those thoughts away.

"Come with me," her mother said in an even tone. "Magdalene wants to see you."

The hairs on Willa's neck stood on end at those words.

No, Willa thought. Meeting the Spirit Witch wasn't on her list of things to do that day.

CHAPTER 3

THE WINDING PATHWAY through the woods was barely visible beneath the darkness of the trees. The tall oaks seemed to block out almost all traces of light. That which did shine through only highlighted the roses that grew all along this part of the woods.

Willa followed behind her mother, her hands folded before her, her head held high. It was a struggle to fake courage in the face of what terror awaited them in the Spirit Witch's castle.

To think that it would soon be passed down to Willa for safe keeping only made her heart beat faster.

Why did she have to be chosen for such a responsibility?

"Keep up," Lady Avery whispered. "The path changes if you aren't paying attention."

Willa's eyes widened. "Really?"

"Yes. If you don't stay close to me, the path is likely to enchant you and lead you to the edge of a cliff."

With a gasp, Willa quickened her speed until she was nearly touching her mother's back. She did want to hold her hand. But that was simply not done. Not anymore. Childish fears and habits would have to be put away.

The path opened to a shiny black gate that appeared before them in the center of the woods. What was once crowded trees and rose bushes, was now a slick white-washed courtyard with a narrow castle that stretched high into the clouds.

Willa swallowed and looked to her mother. "Remarkable."

Instead of replying, Lady Avery turned to Willa and gave her hands a quick squeeze. Something in Lady Avery's sky-blue eyes worried Willa. It was as if she peered into a mirror, her own reflection staring back at her. They shared the same black hair, blue eyes, and porcelain white skin. Her mother, however, had lashes that curled, while Willa's were long and straight. Mother also had a scar that was cleverly hidden by creams and face paints crafted by the best artisans in Paris.

All Willa knew about the scar was that it was caused by a demon.

That was all she needed to know.

"Aren't you coming?" Willa chewed her bottom lip and glanced at the castle. How the clouds were thick and gray at the very top was beyond her, while it was a clear, sunny day just beyond the woods.

Lady Avery shook her head. "I cannot. You must go alone."

Willa tensed. "You didn't tell me that."

"Do not worry. The Spirit Witch will not harm you. You will be fine. And, I will be here at the gate, waiting for your return. We will go home, and talk about that invitation you hid."

Willa cracked a side smirk. "You promised to stop reading my mind…"

Lady Avery smiled back at her. She pinched her cheek, much like she did when Willa was a little girl. "I'm sorry," she whispered. "Bad habits, I suppose."

The screeching of the gate made them both jump, as it opened outward, nearly scrapping them with the double doors. They moved back and waited for the gate to fully open.

"Go now, Willa. Do not show fear. You will rule this all in just a year. Remember that."

Willa swallowed another lump in her throat as she stepped inside the courtyard. *What if I don't want to, Mother?"*

"I heard that," Lady Avery said.

When Willa looked back at her mother, she froze at the tears in her eyes.

"You don't have a choice."

Willa's blood ran cold as her mother ran a finger along her scar.

"Someone has to control the evil of this world. I wasn't strong enough. But," she said, closing her eyes. "You are. You have to be."

Willa opened her mouth to reply, stunned by this sudden revelation, when the gate slammed shut and her mother's image vanished with a haze of fog. With a gasp, Willa ran to the gate and wrapped her hands around the bars.

"Mother!"

There was no reply, just the soft hum of the wind that wrapped around her, chilling her cheeks.

Mother was gone, and it was just Willa, the fog, and the creepy castle at her back.

Spinning around to face her fate, her evergreen dress swished around her legs. A faint outline of a thin woman stood out in the darkness. Her white skin was almost translucent, her white hair almost reaching her knees.

Without a word, the woman turned and entered the castle.

Willa's breaths quickened as she realized that was her cue to follow the Spirit Witch. She forced her feet forward, and tilted her chin upward.

Regal.

Brave.

You are the most powerful witch in the European coven, she told herself as the creases in her forehead relaxed. *Act like it.*

She'd practiced this face for what seemed her entire life.

A queen must never show weakness, mother would say.

The bubbling in her belly betrayed her façade. Good thing no way could see her insides. Two statues stood at either end of the main entrance. One was an angel, with its wings wrapped around its body like a shield, it's sword pointed to the sky. The other was a demon, crouched low to the ground, eyeing the angel with its dark stone eyes.

For a moment, she expected the demon to shift its gaze, and glare her way. Shivering, Willa kept her eyes averted and walked up the slick, stone steps. The light that came from deep inside the entrance only mildly comforted her.

She had to step into the tall doors all alone.

The Spirit Room. It awaited her arrival.

One last glance back at the gate did little to soothe her nerves. Willa didn't think she'd ever wanted her mother by her side more than that moment.

Why the Spirit Witch wanted her so soon was vexing.

Did they really think she was ready?

Inside, Willa covered her exposed arms. A chill in the air startled her.

"Apologies, Willa," a soft voice said from behind her.

Willa stiffened and glanced over her shoulder. The Spirit Witch stood there as the doors closed on their own.

She was beautiful. Of course. Willa expected nothing less. If a Caster was going to be immortal, they were going to maintain their beauty while doing so. Willa had yet to come face to face with an ugly witch. It was just one of the many gifts of being bestowed such power. Though, they did have their share of curses.

With thin green eyes that had an upward slant, the Spirit Witch had taut skin and the appearance of a girl of eighteen.

Something about her beauty comforted Willa, even though she knew what was to come.

"Have you been well?"

Willa nodded, and watched as the Spirit Witch walked before her in a shapeless black dress that hung long to her ankles. The flickering light behind the Spirit Witch was distracting, seeming to dance and grow brighter and brighter.

It was a fire, crackling so loudly that the sound echoed throughout the empty castle.

Clearing her throat, Willa glanced upward to the second level where there was nothing but darkness.

"I've been well, thank you, Spirit Witch."

"Call me Magdalena. We are sisters. No need for formal titles," Magdalena said with a small grin. She looked Willa up and down. "At least not yet. When you are queen, I shall refer to you as such. Until then, you are simply my darling student, Willa Avery."

"Yes, Magdalena," Willa said, returning the smile. Comforted by the student and teacher dynamic, Willa relaxed. If there was one thing she enjoyed above all, it was the quest for knowledge. Proficient in mathematics, science, history, and an assortment of classical languages, Willa was a scholar worthy of the highest accolades. Soon, she would embark on her first semester in college, a journey she'd dreamed of since childhood.

Now, she just needed to learn one more thing. The one thing her mother or her grandmother could never master.

How to tame a demon.

CHAPTER 4

ix Weeks Later
        THE DARGAARD BALL was more opulent than Willa
        could have dreamed. Dressed in a rich red gown with a golden sash tied tightly around her thin waist, and golden shoes with a single strap, all eyes landed on Willa as she and her mother and father entered the ball room. She was especially proud of the golden ribbon tied around her hair, securing her bangs and thick dark hair. A gift from her grandmother, she found any excuse to wear it.

Tonight was the perfect night. Willa was on the hunt for a potential husband...and only one young man would do.

Willa's eyes widened at the amount of people present. It seemed that the entire town of Cambridgeshire and the surrounding villages were there in their finest, with eagerness on their faces to see the mysterious new family in town. Willa could relate. She scanned the crowd for a glimpse of Kristoff or her many brothers. They were all handsome. But, there was something special about the youngest. An assortment of country folk, lords and ladies, and to Willa's surprise, royalty crowded the Dargaard Manor.

"Looks like Lady Catherine and her minions are here," Willa's mother whispered to her father.

Willa grinned. Six weeks ago she might have been afraid of Lady Catherine and her four daughters, and twin nieces. They were from the Lester family, the only line of witches even close to the Averys.

Still, Willa could meet their eyes with confidence. Her final test had been completed.

No one could touch her now.

"Please do behave yourself, Anna," Willa's father, Lord William Avery said just before yawning.

Poor father, Willa thought with an inward chuckle. *Dragged out on one of our schemes again.*

Willa's mother hid a grin. "I shall try, my love."

"Very well," Lord Avery said. "I'll be in the study with Lord Dargaard and his *minions*."

Willa laughed and she and her mother curtsied as he walked toward the side hallway off of the main hall that led into the ballroom.

Now that they were alone, Willa's mother leaned in close to her. "Now, darling. Let's find that man of yours."

Willa nodded, and together they entered the fray. The way country folk reacted to lords and ladies was flattering. You'd have thought they were royalty by the showering of compliments and praise Willa and her mother received as they passed each group of women. Lady Catherine, however, simply gave them a nod of respect. Despite their differences, they were in the same coven. No matter what, if it came down to a fight between the humans and the witches, Lady Catherine and her girls would be by Willa and her mother's side.

But, for now, they kept their distance.

"Lady Avery," Mrs. Pratt said, with a tug on Anna Avery's sleeve.

Lady Avery shot a glare at the middle-aged woman, but kept her voice calm. "Yes? Did you need something?"

Mrs. Pratt's face reddened as she withdrew her hand as if it were on fire. She stumbled over her words. "Yes, ma'am. I mean, my lady. Please forgive my lack of decorum. I just wanted to see if you remembered that my daughter, Emma is going Girton College with young Willa."

Willa smiled at Emma Pratt, a fair redhead with freckles that gave her an undeniable charm. While they'd never spoken more than a few words to one another, Willa did look forward to having someone she knew around once she departed for her first year of college.

"I do," Lady Avery said, glancing at Emma with disinterest.

"Very good," Mrs. Pratt said, nervously. She took in a deep breath, as if searching for courage.

Willa wished she could soothe the woman's nerves, but she knew how intimidating her mother could be.

"Perhaps they can be confidants there. I know Mr. Pratt and I are awfully worried about her leaving us. Aren't you worried about Willa?"

"No," Lady Avery said, cooly. "I am not. But, I am sure Willa would be happy to befriend your eldest."

"Oh," Mrs. Pratt said, lighting up. "Thank you, Lady Avery. We can arrange a lunch or something."

"Very well. Good evening," Lady Avery said, her attention diverted. She took Willa by the hand and they left Mrs. Pratt and her eager daughter.

Willa raised a brow as her mother led her away. "What is it?"

Lady Avery glanced at her. "Kristoff," she said. "He's right this way."

Butterflies filled Willa's stomach. After all of her imaginings of a romantic relationship with the young man, she was now nervous about coming face to face with him again.

Right, she thought. Queen's face. *Use that, and you'll be fine.*

She relaxed her facial muscles and exhaled. Talking to a man should be the last thing she feared.

But, when their eyes met from across the piano, she nearly stumbled.

"Are you all right?"

Willa nodded.

"Silly girl. He adores you," Lady Avery said. "I should know."

Willa's brow creased. "Mother, stop reading his mind," she said between clenched teeth.

Lady Avery chuckled, and stroked the back of Willa's hand. "Habit, my love. Habit."

Slightly annoyed that her mother knew more about Kristoff and his thoughts than she did, she followed her anyway. With sandy brown hair cut short on the sides and left long on the top, and bright green eyes, Kristoff stood out from the other men at the ball. He and his family wore their Norwegian style of dress, which wasn't terribly different from the English, but intriguing nonetheless. In a black suit with a long jacket and white vest over an evergreen shirt, he was as dapper as ever.

One charming, white smile directed her way, and Willa forgot everything she'd planned to say.

No one else seemed to matter or exist as she approached the man she'd been dreaming about since their first encounter in town weeks ago.

She smiled back at him as he bowed to her. Willa curtsied with a slight bow to her head.

"Lady Anna Avery and Lady Willa Avery," Kristoff said, still smiling as if he knew a joke but didn't want to share.

Willa wished she could read his thoughts.

"Good day, Lord Dargaard," Willa said as he took her hand and kissed her knuckles. With his touch, her smile wavered as a surge of cold filled her veins. She'd have expected heat, but the cold was refreshing, rejuvenating.

He winked at her. "I'm pleased that you were able to make it."

"We wouldn't dream of missing it," Lady Avery said. "Speaking of dreaming, I need to speak to your dear mother. She mentioned having trouble sleeping at our last luncheon. I may have a remedy for her."

Kristoff nodded. "Lovely. She and my sisters are toward the back of the hall." He leaned in and whispered. "They like to linger near the table of cakes."

Willa covered her mouth as a laugh escaped her lips. Her mother left them to seek out the Dargaard women. She wondered what potion she planned on giving Kristoff's mother, but the way he looked at her was more pressing at the moment.

"So," Kristoff began, moving closer to Willa, so close that she couldn't help but blush. He whispered into her ear, causing her skin to heat and her eyes to flutter closed. "Now that we are all alone, who is going to protect you from me, now?"

CHAPTER 5

CHILLS RAN UP Willa's exposed skin at Kristoff's remark. No man had ever spoken to her in such a manner. For a moment, she was left speechless.

He laughed at her, and rubbed his chin with his knuckles. "I didn't mean to offend you, my lady," he said.

Willa cleared her throat and looked from side to side. Everyone stared at them. The whispers. She heard them loud and clearly. She knew what the other guests were thinking, how they probably envied her for capturing the attention of one of the most eligible bachelors in the county.

Instead of showing her embarrassment, Willa leaned right into him and narrowed her eyes. "No, sir. You're alone with *me*."

Kristoff's eyes widened. An amused smile came to his lips. "Well," he said, folding his hands behind his back. "In that case, let's say we enjoy the night air."

Willa grinned and extended her arm. "Shall we?"

With Kristoff's arm locked around hers, Willa and Kristoff attracted more attention as they left the main ballroom and exited to the garden.

"You're not worried someone will think it improper?"

Willa glanced at Kristoff. "A lady can have a conversation with a gentleman in the presence of others," she said, nodding to the scant groups of ladies and gentlemen enjoying the gas lamps set around the back courtyard. "Besides, my family cares little about what others think. We run this county, if you haven't heard."

Kristoff lifted a brow. "I see. The Avery's are in for a bit of competition."

"Is that so?" Willa paused at the edge of the stairs that led down to a white path that stretched far into the horizon, past the rectangular pond, exquisite shrubbery designs, and lamps that lit the way.

"Why? Are you worried?"

Willa's blood ran cold as she peered at the night sky. It was a clear evening, with stars that shone as bright as the full moon. Her heart thumped in her chest as the scent of something unnatural came to her on the soft breeze.

The scent was unmistakable. It was the one thing that made Willa want to gag.

Blood.

Willa's right eye twitched. Every fiber of her body ignited with warnings as she stood there, desperate for answers as to what awaited in the darkness below.

"Willa?"

Kristoff's voice was too far away to grab her attention. Not now. She inhaled, deeply, and closed her eyes.

"Kelser," Willa whispered inside her head. A light shone in the darkness of her subconscious. Like a candle, it wavered and flickered like the fire in the Spirt Witch's castle, soon to be her new home. What she'd seen in the Spirit Room would never fade from her memory. While terrifying, she could draw strength from it.

"Illias," Willa called, and another light joined that of Kelser's.

In unison, her soul familiars answered. *Yes, Master?*

When Willa opened her eyes, all she saw was blood and the dead bodies of the partygoers.

A premonition.

If she didn't act quickly, her vision would become reality.

"Find it," she hissed aloud. "Find it, now."

Someone grabbed Willa by the arm, waking her from her trance.

"Willa?"

Kristoff's looked down at her, worry in his eyes. She realized that he held her up by her arms. Shaking her head, she removed herself from his grasp.

"Are you all right? Shall I call the doctor?"

"No," Willa said, more forcefully than she'd intended. Before she could speak another word, her soul familiars returned, slamming into her body with such force that she had to grip Kristoff to keep herself steady.

"What is wrong?"

"*Vampires*," Kelser and Illias said in unison. "*Two.*"

Willa's eyes widened, and she kicked off her shoes. With one glance back at Kristoff, she licked her lips and shook her head. "I wish I could tell you."

Then, she ran down the stairs, her dress bunched in her fists to keep from tripping on the lace fabric at the hem. As she ran down the stairs and to the pathway, she suddenly wished she'd have told her mother and perhaps the Lesters.

There were nine witches on the grounds, two of which were Elite Casters. Whoever the vampires were, they picked the wrong party to crash.

Yet, Willa ran headfirst to defeat them.

Alone.

The hush of the night filled her ears as she focused on deciphering where the vampires were. The thought that they were in her territory enraged her.

Her land. Her people. Didn't they know any better?

Something caught her attention from the trees to her left. Willa froze, her heightened senses alert.

Thuds on the ground. She could feel the vibration beneath her bare feet.

Running. She lifted a brow. Someone was running. Very fast.

At that thought, something ran into her and lifted her from the ground. Willa's mouth opened as the wind was knocked out of her. Whatever had her, pushed her across the garden and into the trees on the other side of the grounds. A whoosh of cool air slapped her face as she flew through the air, and was slammed into the grass.

"Well," a female voice hissed. "Don't you look delicious."

It took a moment for Willa to regain her vision. The blow to the back of her head made her dizzy as she sat up.

The vampire placed a foot on Willa's chest, pressing her into the dirt.

Willa coughed and struggled to see who stood above her.

"Frightening, isn't it? You'll never see my face. It's a little trick I just learned."

The vampire reeked of blood. As she knelt down to bring her face close to Willa's the stench intensified.

"What's this?" A male voice called from the shadows.

Willa's head lolled to the right to see him. With swarthy skin and long black hair, Willa had never seen the vampire before. How could she? They didn't come out during the day, and she'd never seen him at an evening event. The lilt in his accent hinted that he was Italian.

"Marco. You're still too slow."

"Do not tease me," Marco replied. "What do you have there?"

"Our second course of the evening, love," the female said with a chuckle as she sniffed Willa's neck. "Come, smell her. She is divine."

Give me strength, Willa whispered to Kelser and Illias.

Yes, Master.

With that, a surge of energy flooded Willa's body. She grabbed the vampire by her hair and rose from the ground and to her feet. Hovering in the air, Willa held onto the vampire and met the gaze of her male companion.

"Gesù Cristo," Marco said.

Jesus Christ? Willa shot him a glance. "A vampire, calling for Jesus Christ? He cannot save you today."

"Stop," the female said. "Who are you?"

"Willa Avery, Grand Elite Caster, future queen of the European coven, future delegate of witch affairs for the Netherworld Division."

"Jesus Christ is right," the female said. "Please. We didn't know."

Willa pulled her up to eye level. "How did you not know? This is Elite Caster territory, and we do not tolerate death to any human or witch within our borders."

She nodded, tears in her eyes. Willa could finally get a glimpse of the vampire's face as whatever power she'd used waned. She had dark brown hair, and brown eyes that matched Marco's. Realization that they weren't lovers hit Willa.

They were siblings.

"Please. I beg of you. We were just turned days ago. No one taught us the rules," she whined. "We didn't ask for this."

Willa's brows lifted. "Days ago?"

Both young vampires nodded. "We are waiting for our master to come back for us. We were hungry. But, he is cruel, and he wishes to watch us suffer."

The way her self-assured demeanor shifted to that of a scolded child turned Willa's stomach. How could she kill them knowing they truly didn't know the rules set between humans and vampires? The Netherworld Division must be notified, as well as her coven.

Willa sensed that dark times were on the horizon.

"Leave," Willa ordered while the vampire struggled to free her hair from her tight grasp. "If I see you again, or hear of any trespassing, I will be forced to hunt you down and execute you both."

With that, she dropped the vampire to the ground, and within seconds, they ran as fast as the wind the other way they'd came.

Lowering herself back to the ground, Willa straightened her dress. It was no use, grass and dirt had smeared her lovely red satin and lace. She frowned at the hole in her hem.

"Willa," a voice called from behind.

Stiffening, Willa's face drained of color. She slowly turned to look behind her.

There, in the trees, stood Kristoff.

The look of disbelief on his face left her desperate to run away.

"Kristoff," she said, breathing his name in a whisper. "How long have you been there?"

Kristoff emerged from the darkness of the trees and stood before her. Willa shook as she awaited his response. It took an eternity as she watched him rake his hands through his hair, start to speak, then snap his mouth shut. He finally looked down at her and shook his head. For a moment, it seemed that he read her soul.

If he had, he would have run away as quickly as he could.

"Kristoff?"

He sighed and took her hands into his. "I saw it all. Heard it all."

Tears welled in her eyes. So much for a kind and handsome husband worthy of uniting with her family. At the least, so much for a new friend.

"I'm sorry," she whispered.

Instead of turning away from her, he stroked her cheeks and wiped away her tears.

"No," he said, softly. "Do not apologize?"

Willa opened her eyes. "Why?"

Kristoff kissed her forehead. "Because, I want to know everything. I want to know all there is to know about Willa Avery, the girl my father is currently arranging a marriage with."

Those words reached a dark piece of Willa's soul and brightened it. The smile that came to her lips seemed to take over her face.

"Really? Are you certain?"

He nodded. "Yes," said, smiling. "Really."

The quiet of the night gave Willa more courage than she'd had at the start of the evening. She rose on her toes and pressed her lips onto Kristoff's.

With his arms wrapped around her, and the taste of his mouth, Willa realized that more than her power and resolve for fighting evil had been awakened that night.

A small spark deep within her heart was awakened, and she feared it would never slumber.

ACKNOWLEDGMENTS

I would like to thank a few key people in my life. First, my faerie-godmother Colleen Albert. She is my constant inspiration and encourages me in all aspects of my personal life and writing career. I am forever in her debt for years of kindness and love.

Second, I would like to thank Kellie Sheridan for seeing my potential before I had accomplished anything of note.

I'd also like to thank Concierge Literary for making my amazing cover. It's beautiful!

And, lastly, this is for all of my fans around the world who stand by my side and join me on this epic adventure into what is my dream come true.

Thank you.

ABOUT THE AUTHOR

K.N. Lee is a New York Times and USA Today bestselling author who resides in Charlotte, North Carolina. When she is not writing twisted tales, fantasy novels, and dark poetry, she does a great deal of traveling and promotes other authors. Wannabe rockstar, foreign language enthusiast, and anime geek, K.N. Lee also enjoys helping others reach their writing and publishing goals. She is a winner of the Elevate Lifestyle Top 30 Under 30 "Future Leaders of Charlotte" award.

She is signed with Captive Quill Press and Patchwork Press.
(Amazon Author Page)
Join my street team!
facebook.com/groups/1439982526289524/

For more information
www.knlee.com

ALSO BY K.N. LEE

The Dragon Born Saga:

Half-Blood Dragon

Magic-Born Dragon

Queen of the Dragons

War of the Dragons

Fate of the Dragons

Curse of the Dragons

The Chronicles of Koa Series:

Netherworld

Dark Prophet

Blood Princess

The Eura Chronicles:

Rise of the Flame

Night of the Storm

Dawn of the Forgotten (Coming Soon)

Prophecy of the Seer (Coming Soon)

THE GRAND ELITE CASTER TRILOGY:

Silenced

Summoned (Coming Soon)

Sacrificed (Coming Soon)

FORBIDDEN MAGIC:

Court of Shadows

Court of Dragons

Court of Elves

THE FALLEN GODS TRILOGY:

Goddess of War

Goddess of Ruin (Coming Soon)

Queen of Chaos (Coming Soon)

STANDALONE NOVELLAS:

The Scarlett Legacy

Liquid Lust

Spell Slinger

Academia of the Beast

Lost in Laguna

CPSIA information can be obtained
at www.ICGtesting.com
Printed in the USA
BVHW031339040720
582975BV00001B/18